Match Wits with Super Sleuth Nancy Drew!

Collect the Original
Nancy Drew Mystery Stories
by Carolyn Keene

Available in Hardcover!

Celebrate 60 Years with the World's Best Detective!

MYSTERY OF THE GLOWING EYE

When Nancy Drew eagerly agrees to help her lawyer father solve the mystery of the glowing eye, she has no way of knowing that it will involve the kidnapping of her close friend Ned Nickerson.

A puzzling note in Ned's handwriting sets Nancy and her friends Bess and George on a hazardous search for a bizarre criminal. From their base of operations, the Emerson College campus, the three girl detectives and Ned's college pals follow a maze of clues to locate the kidnapper's hideout and rescue Ned. Not only is Nancy greatly worried about Ned, but also she is alarmed by the high-handed methods of a woman lawyer who tries to take the case away from her.

Every reader will thrill to Nancy's exciting adventures as she unravels this dangerous web of mystery.

The force knocked Nancy against the wall.

Mystery of the Glowing Eye

BY CAROLYN KEENE

Publishers • New York
A member of The Putnam & Grosset Group

PRINTED ON RECYCLED PAPER

Contents

CHAPTER I

Runaway Helicopter

THE hall telephone rang persistently. Nancy Drew, however, sat in the living room, lost in thought.

"What did Marty King mean by her remark?" the young detective mused.

Absentmindedly Nancy arose and went to the phone. It had stopped ringing and now no one was on the line.

"Oh dear! The call may have been important!" Nancy chided herself. Then, hoping the caller would try again, she sat down on the chair near the telephone table.

At once her mind reverted to Marty King. The twenty-four-year-old platinum blond was a recent graduate of nearby Bushwick Law School. She was working in Mr. Drew's office as a researcher.

"And not as a detective!" Nancy fumed. "She can't take the Anderson case away from me!"

The telephone rang again. Nancy's close friend Bess Marvin was calling.

"Hi!" said Nancy. "Have you been trying to get me?"

"No. Why?"

Nancy replied, "How about you and George coming over? I'll tell you why. I can't leave the house because Dad is expecting a new letter file to be delivered for his den, and I'm alone here."

The two girls arrived shortly. They were cousins and often assisted Nancy in her detective work. The three girls were a striking trio— Nancy, an attractive, slender, strawberry blond; Bess, a dimpled, blue-eyed blond, slightly overweight; and George Fayne, who enjoyed her boyish name and had short dark hair and a slim, straight figure.

"What's worrying you, Nancy?" Bess asked. "On the phone you sounded as if something horrible had happened."

"It's not that bad," Nancy replied, forcing a smile. "I guess it's a case of just plain jealousy."

"You jealous?" George scoffed. "That's one trait you don't have. Well, out with it!"

"It's about a young woman named Marty King who has recently come to work for Dad. She's a lawyer."

"Uh-uh!" Bess said with a little giggle. "You think she has a romantic interest in your dad, and/or vice versa."

Nancy was startled by the suggestion and hastened to assure her friends this was not the situation. "Marty King is trying to be an amateur detective—"

"And," George finished, "take your place."

Nancy nodded. "Dad mentioned he has a case he thought I'd like to work on with you girls. It's about a glowing eye."

"Glowing eye!" George echoed. "Sounds intriguing."

"Yes," Nancy agreed. "But this morning Marty called me and said I wouldn't need to help—that she already had partly solved the case."

"The nerve of her!" George burst out. "What did your father say?"

"I haven't told him," Nancy replied. "And what's more, I'm not going to. Maybe he asked Marty to take over and—"

"Don't be silly," Bess cut in. "I'm sure your dad would never do such a thing."

Nancy wanted to believe this was true. But as Bess tried to console her friend, the young detective's thoughts drifted off. Would her father ever again discuss with her the cases that troubled him? What would it be like without a mystery for her to solve?

Tears formed in Nancy's eyes, but she smiled and said, "Thank you, Bess. Maybe I'm just making a mountain out of a molehill."

George put an arm about Nancy's shoulder.

"Or maybe Miss King thinks she's a queen!" With a broad grin, George added, "Which mystery does my lady wish to solve today? Or shall we slay the wicked dragon—?"

"Enough, enough," Nancy interrupted, though she could not refrain from laughing at the pompous expression on George's face.

Paying no attention to her friend's remark, George bowed deeply. "Your Highness," she said, brandishing an imaginary sword at her cousin.

"Your *Low*-ness," Bess replied. "How low will you go?"

George bent over so far that she lost her balance and fell forward. "Is that low enough?" she said, resting on her elbows and looking up into Bess's dimpled smile.

At that instant the three girls became aware of a loud whirring noise. It grew louder.

"That sounds like a copter!" Nancy exclaimed. "And it's right overhead!"

She dashed out the front door with her friends and looked up. A small twin-motor helicopter was descending.

"Nancy, it's going to land on your front lawn!" George cried out, and Bess ran back inside the house.

Nancy and George watched in fascination. The rotors suddenly stopped and the helicopter plummeted the last fifty feet. It hit the grass with a thud and the door flew open.

"Nancy, it's going to land on your lawn!"
George cried out.

"The pilot!" Nancy exclaimed. "He must have been injured!"

She and George hurried to the helicopter. They could not see the pilot, so the two girls climbed up and peered inside.

No one was there!

By this time Bess had run out and joined the others. "I called the police. Was anyone hurt?" When she heard that the craft was a pilotless helicopter, she stared in amazement. "Are you sure?" she asked.

"Not a soul here," Nancy reported with a bewildered shrug.

The young detective, hoping to find a clue to the missing pilot, hopped aboard.

Nancy picked up an envelope which lay on the floor, face down. She turned it over. Her eyes opened wide in disbelief. The name on it was her own! There was no address.

"Did you find something?" George called up.

Nancy jumped down and showed her friends the sealed envelope. The handwriting, which they all recognized immediately, was that of her special friend Ned Nickerson. For a moment she could not speak.

But finally she said, "Perhaps Ned was in the copter and had to bail out!"

Bess and George were alarmed too. All of them were extremely fond of the good-looking Emerson College student. Arm in arm the three girls walked back into the house.

"Open the envelope," Bess urged. "Maybe it contains a message for you."

Nancy, who had been clutching the envelope tightly, slid her thumb under the flap. Inside was a small piece of paper. On it was a handwritten warning:

Beware of Cyclops.
Ned

CHAPTER II

A Suspected Forgery

NANCY sat dazed and bewildered. Bess, overcome by the thought of a tragedy, was wiping tears from her eyes.

George was the first to speak. "We mustn't think the worst. Maybe Ned wasn't in the copter. The note might have been planted by someone else."

Before the others could comment, the girls became aware that the police as well as neighbors had arrived. They were swarming over the large front lawn of the Drews' colonial brick house. A photographer was snapping pictures and several officers were taking turns climbing into the helicopter to examine it.

As Nancy and Bess emerged from the house, there were shouts from the crowd. "What happened?" "Was anybody hurt?" "Nancy, is this a publicity stunt?"

Many times since she had solved her first case, *The Secret of the Old Clock,* until her most recent one, *The Double Jinx Mystery,* the young detective had been in the public eye. But she herself tried to avoid publicity.

A police officer began to question her about the helicopter. Nancy answered that she had no idea who the owner was. She did not mention the note she had found because she wanted to discuss it with her friend Chief McGinnis and also her father before revealing its contents.

Another officer came up and reported there was no clue to the owner in the helicopter. The only identification was the registration number under the tail rotor. He said he would have headquarters find out from the FAA the name of the person to whom the number had been assigned.

As he went off to use his car radio, George emerged from the house. She took Nancy aside and said, "I did some checking by phone at Emerson. Ned wasn't at any of the usual places he goes, and an Omega Chi Epsilon brother at his fraternity house said there was a rumor that Ned had been kidnapped the day before!"

"Kidnapped!" Bess shrieked. At once all eyes turned on her.

"*Sh!*" Nancy cautioned. "What exactly did you find out, George?"

"I asked to speak to Burt." Burt Eddleton was a special friend of George's. "Ned told the boy on duty at the house he was taking a drive. When he didn't return, Dave and Burt went looking for him." Dave Evans was a boy Bess dated. "They found Ned's car abandoned on a road near Emerson. Thinking that possibly something had gone wrong with the car and Ned had left to get help, the boys had looked it over. The car seemed to be in perfect condition."

Nancy went into the house and sat down in the living room. She felt weak. Ned kidnapped! But why?

Suddenly a thought came to her and she pulled his note from her pocket. "This may be a forgery!"

Nancy examined the writing carefully. If it was forged, the writing was a clever imitation. The words had been hastily penciled. Another thought came to her. Had Ned written "Beware of Cyclops" of his own volition or had he been forced to do so?

Many fantastic ideas ran through Nancy's mind. Was Ned warning her about a possible gang called Cyclops, or was someone trying to scare her?

"The message could have been telegraphed," Nancy said to herself. "If Ned wanted to reach me in a hurry, a telegram or phone call would have been faster—unless he was confined in some way.

"It's even possible," Nancy thought, "that if Ned is being held somewhere, this is a clue to his whereabouts."

Just then Mr. Drew walked in with Police Chief McGinnis. The tall, handsome lawyer and the rugged, ruddy-faced officer looked concerned.

"Nancy, what's happened?" her father exclaimed.

Before answering, Nancy turned to Bess and George. "Will you girls keep everyone away from here while I talk to Dad and the chief?"

The cousins hurried outside. The police were already ordering curious men, women, and children from the front lawn of the house. There was a short confrontation with a photographer who insisted upon entering to take Nancy's picture, but the girls were firm.

"No pictures, please," George told him and finally the young man agreed. He turned and followed the crowd to the street.

Meanwhile, Nancy had started to tell the story of the helicopter, the strange note, and Ned's disappearance to the chief and her father. She showed them the envelope and its contents, and said she was sure the handwriting was Ned's.

"Chief McGinnis," she asked, "have you ever heard of a person or an organization called Cyclops?"

The officer shook his head. "Never. But I'll call

headquarters and check on it." He went to the phone and came back in a few minutes to report there was no such name on record.

"Nancy," said her father, "what's your theory about the whole thing?"

"Frankly, I have none yet," she replied. "I'm too worried about Ned. Was he held up? Drugged? Or enticed away by a phony message?"

Chief McGinnis looked grave. "If no one gets word of him soon, I'll report this to the FBI, unless the Emerson police have already done so. I'll find out."

Nancy spoke up. "May I keep the note?"

The officer smiled. "Since it is a personal message addressed to you and found on the premises of your home, which is private property, I guess the note belongs to you. But I'd like to have it for a while, at least."

Mr. Drew put in, "Suppose I make a photostat in my office, then give you the original."

"Oh, let me do it!" Nancy said quickly. She had a mental picture of Marty King seeing the note and asking Mr. Drew about it. If he told her of the strange events connected with it, she might try to involve herself in the case. Nancy's father looked surprised, but she added hastily, "I want to keep this a secret, Dad."

"All right. You drive down to the office and make the copy yourself."

One of the policemen came in to say a message

for the chief had been received over his car radio. "A report just came in that no parachutists have been found in the area."

After he went outside, Chief McGinnis said, "What puzzles me is how the copter was flown here."

Nancy made a guess. "Maybe it's a robot copter. And someone deliberately sent it here to deliver the message. Of course that's quite an elaborate way to do so."

"And how is the owner going to get back his copter?" the chief asked. "We don't know where it came from."

"Wherever the place is, I'll bet that's where Ned is being held," Nancy answered. She looked grim. "Let's go out and see if we can get a soil clue from the tires."

By this time the crowd in the street had dispersed and only the police were left. Nancy had brought her magnifying glass. An examination of the dried mud on the tires indicated that the take-off spot was probably near a swamp of black muck. She found tiny shreds of wood in it. "A lumber camp, or some other kind of forest area," the young detective murmured to herself.

Without warning the engine burst into life and the rotors began to whir.

"The copter's getting ready to leave!" Nancy cried out. "I must go with it. Maybe it will take me to Ned." She began to climb aboard.

Mr. Drew jumped forward and made a grab for his daughter. "No!" he shouted. "It's too dangerous! If the copter is controlled by an enemy, the operator could kidnap you and even kill you!"

Chief McGinnis agreed with Mr. Drew and added his caution. Before Nancy could step down, the rotors suddenly stopped whirring and the engine became silent.

"Something went wrong!" George exclaimed.

"Thank goodness," said Bess. "Otherwise Nancy might be up in the air and off on a dangerous mission!"

Nancy nodded, but was more interested in the helicopter. "It must be remote-controlled," she commented, "and can take off and land at any time."

"But why did its engine stop?" Bess asked.

Nancy assumed that the operator had used a sensitized gadget which let him know whenever there was added weight in the helicopter, indicating that someone was aboard uninvited.

"We'll prevent it from flying away," said the chief. "Tomorrow the police will take it. Girls, would you find some heavy pieces for my men to pile inside? I want to keep the copter here if possible until we can check on its ownership and move it."

While the husky police chief and a few of his officers clung to the craft, Nancy and her father hurried into the garage and brought out a heavy tire rim, an iron bucket left by a painter, and part of an unused steel fence as ballast.

"That should help," the chief said.

George had a suggestion. "Why don't we tie the copter down? I saw a lot of strong, thick rope in the garage."

The others agreed and the craft was securely anchored to a tall, sturdy-looking tree. Bess and George said they must leave but would be back in the morning to help Nancy on the case. Chief McGinnis ordered one man to stay on duty. He and the rest drove off.

As Nancy and her father started for the front door, their housekeeper, Mrs. Hannah Gruen, arrived in a taxi. She alighted and stared in astonishment at the helicopter, then at the Drews. Mrs. Gruen, middle-aged, and adored by Nancy, had lived with the Drews since the death of Nancy's mother when the girl was only three years old.

Mr. Drew smiled. "We had a robot visitor," he told the housekeeper. "Nancy will tell you the whole story. I must run back to the office, but I'll be home by ten tonight. Please call Miss King and tell her I'm returning."

Nancy made no comment. The last thing in the world she wanted to do was talk to Marty King. She turned to Hannah. "Will you do it, please?"

Unaware of Nancy's reason for the request, the housekeeper made the call, then went to the kitchen to start dinner preparations.

Nancy followed. "Don't cook much for me. I'm not hungry."

"Why, what's the matter, dear?" Hannah asked.

"Lots of things. But worst of all, we think Ned has been kidnapped."

"What!"

Nancy explained and ended by saying, "I want to find Ned, but I don't know which direction to go."

"That's not like you," the housekeeper said kindly. "You've had a bad shock, dear. I suggest you eat a simple dinner and go right to bed. In the morning you'll be refreshed and ready to start on the case."

"But which case?" Nancy asked. "Ned, the robot copter, Cyclops, the glowing eye—"

"Stop!" Mrs. Gruen exclaimed. "That's three too many. Nancy, do be sensible. Why not concentrate on Ned? Call Burt or Dave and see if there's any news."

Nancy took Hannah's advice and went to the phone. Burt answered quickly, hoping the police were calling to report a clue to Ned's whereabouts. He told Nancy there was no news from or about Ned.

"Have Mr. and Mrs. Nickerson been notified?" Nancy asked.

"Yes, and they haven't heard anything. Apparently you're the only one who received a message."

During dinner Nancy and Hannah discussed the strange happenings of the day, but the young detective refrained from mentioning Marty King and her part in trying to solve the glowing eye mystery.

Later Nancy called the Nickersons, expressed her concern, and told them about the note signed by their son. "Do you know anything about Cyclops?"

"Cyclops? No," Mr. Nickerson replied, and his wife on an extension phone said, "We never heard Ned mention it, so I'm sure it must be some new contact. Oh, Nancy, use your best detective instincts and find him," Ned's mother pleaded.

"I'll do my best," Nancy promised.

By nine-thirty Nancy felt so exhausted she decided not to wait for her father's return, but to go to bed. She soon drifted off into a sound sleep. Several hours later she was awakened by a tremendous racket on the front lawn and jumped out of bed.

Nancy rushed to a window just in time to see the robot helicopter rising from the lawn!

CHAPTER III

A Glowing Eye

By the time Nancy had put on robe and slippers and had run into the hall, her father and Hannah Gruen were already there. Without a word all three rushed down the front stairway and out the door. Mr. Drew switched on a light that flooded the lawn.

The guy ropes which had held the helicopter down now lay on the ground. The craft itself was out of sight, but the moving lights in the sky indicated the copter had taken a northeasterly direction.

"That's toward Emerson," Nancy said. Then her thoughts turned to the officer who had been left by the police to watch the helicopter. "Where's the guard?"

He was not in sight and Hannah suggested, "Maybe he was kidnapped too!"

"And possibly taken away in the copter," Mr. Drew added.

Nancy had a different idea. "He may have been knocked out and left behind. Let's look around."

They did not have to search far. The guard was lying unconscious in the Drews' garage. The officer did not respond to their first-aid treatment, so Nancy's father phoned headquarters to report the incident and request medical help.

An ambulance with a police surgeon and a patrol car with two other officers reached the house within minutes. Dr. Tompkin quickly examined the injured guard.

"Dooley got a severe blow on his head. We'll take him to the hospital at once. Probably have to operate."

"That's dreadful!" Mrs. Gruen spoke up.

"Indeed it is, ma'am," said one of the remaining men, who introduced himself as Erman. "And so is all crime. Suppose we go into the house and you tell me what happened here."

Hannah quickly made hot chocolate. As the group sipped it and ate some cookies, Nancy, her father, and the housekeeper told what they knew about the case.

"This sure is a strange one," Erman said. "Of course the thing to do is track down the take-off point of the copter. I'll check with the chief to see if he's put anyone on that angle. Otherwise

we'll start right on it." The two men arose,
thanked Mrs. Gruen for the hot chocolate, and
said good night.

After Mr. Drew had closed the front door, he
smiled fondly at Nancy. "That plan to track the
copter was your idea too, wasn't it?"

Nancy nodded. Then, on a hunch, she changed
the subject. "Dad, you never finished telling me
about the glowing eye."

"No, but I will. It's too late now. We must
all get to bed."

Nancy went to her room, but she kept thinking, "Did Dad mean it was too late because Marty
is working on the case?"

The young detective found it impossible to
sleep. Finally at six o'clock she dressed and drove
to Mr. Drew's office to which she had a key.
Quickly she made a photostat of Ned's note and
put it in her purse. Then she left the original at
police headquarters for Chief McGinnis and
went home.

No one was up yet. Using the telephone extension in the kitchen, she called George, then Bess.

"Will you drive up to Emerson with me today?" she asked. "I want to try getting a lead on
Ned. Could you be ready in an hour?"

Both girls promised to hurry. Nancy ate a cold
breakfast, left a note for her father, then hurried
from the house to pick up George and Bess.

As they headed toward the highway in Nancy's

convertible, Bess asked, "What's the big rush?
Did you pick up a clue?"

Nancy briefed the cousins on the night's happenings. They were thunderstruck and George
asked, "Do you think the copter took off by re-
mote control, or did whoever attacked the police
guard fly it?"

"I don't know," Nancy replied. "Probably the
police will come this morning and investigate."

The girls were silent for nearly two miles as
they enjoyed the early morning with its twitter-
ing birds and hide-and-seek sunshine.

Finally Bess spoke up. "What is Cyclops, anyway? I remember something from school about
it being a one-eyed monster."

"I looked it up to make sure," Nancy replied.
"The story comes from Greek mythology. There
was a race of giant shepherds. Each man had only
one eye. It was in the center of his forehead. The
Cyclops made weapons and armor for the gods,
and also thunderbolts. One of these thunderbolts
killed Aesculapius, so his father Apollo had all
the shepherds put to death."

"What a gruesome story!" Bess commented.
"But what in the world did Ned mean by Cyclops?"

George had no answer, but presently Nancy
said, "I have a hunch that maybe the glowing eye
is a present-day Cyclops."

Bess's eyes opened wide. "You mean there's a

one-eyed monster man loose somewhere? And he kidnaps people?"

"Yes," George replied. "And his main diet is plump young ladies who like to eat sweets."

Bess made a face at her cousin, then said, "Nancy, are you suggesting that Ned is being held by some monster man?"

"With one eye?" George added.

"Seriously," Nancy answered, "Ned may have stumbled upon a clue in the glowing eye mystery. I did mention it to him. Oh, I wish I knew what his note means!"

By eleven o'clock Bess began to complain of being starved. "Let's stop for a bite in Martin City," she suggested.

Though Nancy would have liked to push on and had not thought of food, she suddenly realized she was hungry. "Okay, Bess."

When they reached the turnoff, Nancy took the downhill road that led to the industrial city on the Wimpole River. "What do they manufacture here?" she asked.

George said, "Fresh-water fishing equipment and small boats. My dad has bought a lot of things made by these people. By the way, this is a historic place. Maybe we could look around a little."

"After we eat," Bess said firmly.

At an intersection in town Nancy inquired of a traffic policeman where there was a good restaurant. He recommended The Clearview. In a few minutes the girls reached the attractive, ivy-covered brick homestead. Inside, it was filled with beautiful old furniture and paintings.

"How charming!" Bess exclaimed as the girls went to the powder room.

A few minutes later a headwaitress led them toward a table by the window. Nancy, who was ahead of the others, stopped suddenly. At a booth for two in a secluded corner sat her father and Marty King!

"What's the matter?" asked George, who had bumped into Nancy. The young detective did not answer. Instead she called to the headwaitress. "We'd like to sit back here." She herself chose a table out of sight of her father and his assistant.

After the headwaitress had handed the girls menus and gone off, Nancy told the cousins what had startled her. "I thought it best not to be seen by Dad and Marty," she added.

George guessed what was going through her friend's mind. "You're afraid Marty will think you followed them because she was going to work on the glowing eye mystery."

"Yes," Nancy replied. "And I don't want Marty to bring it up to me. They must have flown here. Let's eat quickly and leave."

The young detective's hopes of not being seen were in vain. A short time later Marty came directly toward the girls on her way to the telephone booth in the hall. She looked surprised, but said cheerily, "Hello, Nancy. How's everything? Have you caught up with the kidnappers yet?"

Nancy introduced Bess and George. Marty smiled, then said, "Oh, you're the girls who help Nancy solve mysteries. What fun you must have! Well, I'll run now and make a call to the office."

She walked away without saying a word about Mr. Drew. On impulse Nancy got up, said to Bess and George, "Order me some soup and a ham on rye," and hurried across the room to speak to her father.

He was surprised but invited her to sit down. "Marty's with me," he said. "We flew up here in connection with a boat-company case. You decided rather suddenly to go to Emerson, didn't you?"

"Yes. It may be a wild-goose chase, but I'm trying to follow the course that copter took. By the way, I think there may be a connection between Cyclops that Ned mentioned and your mystery of the glowing eye. Dad, you haven't yet told me details about that mystery, which you first called the Anderson case."

"You could be right about a connection between the two cases," the lawyer agreed. "I'll tell you the whole story when I have time." Out of the corner of her eye, Nancy saw Marty coming back. "I'll give you this hint. Investigate the

Anderson Museum in Hager. It's about six miles from here."

Nancy returned to her table in a far better mood than she had left it. Her father was not sidestepping her detective work in favor of Marty's after all! Bess and George noticed the difference in their friend. But before they had a chance to ask her about it, Nancy said they were going to Hager to pick up a clue.

"What is it?" George asked.

"Something to do with Cyclops or the glowing eye."

Twenty minutes later the three girls were on their way. Mr. Drew and Marty remained at the restaurant. The six miles were quickly covered.

Hager proved to be another historic town with brownstone mansions dating back to the "elegant eighties" and still in fine condition. Tall trees and well-kept lawns lent the area a picturesque, though severe atmosphere.

Bess remarked, "I wouldn't be happy living in these surroundings. You'd never dare disturb anything, and you'd be afraid to laugh."

Nancy smiled at Bess's pretended fears. "Cheer up. The people here are no doubt very friendly."

After riding around a while the girls came to a large estate with a high hedge around it. Over the entrance drive was a stone archway with a large silver nameplate at the top. Engraved in script was *Anderson Museum*.

Nancy parked and the girls started up the long walk to the museum. There were no flowers, no bright-colored shrubs, just green grass and evergreen trees on either side.

When the visitors reached the building, the huge front door was opened by a slender, elderly woman whose plain black dress and severe hairstyle fitted the rigid surroundings. "Good afternoon," she said, but her face was expressionless.

"I'm Nancy Drew." The young detective smiled. "My father is Carson Drew, a lawyer in River Heights. He suggested I visit your museum." She then introduced Bess and George.

Nancy's smile was not returned. "I'm Miss Wilkin. I don't know your father and we have no lawsuits pending. The only person from River Heights who has been here lately is a Miss King. What in particular do you wish to see?"

Nancy's mind whirled. On a hunch she said quickly, "Just what Miss King saw."

Bess and George could have shouted with excitement but they kept still and followed the straight-backed woman with the uptilted head. She led the girls through a section filled with figures of knights in armor and deadly swords.

"Ugh! I don't like this room," Bess whispered. "It's too scary."

"That is too bad," said Miss Wilkin. "Brave men fighting for their countries used these weapons."

Presently they came to the most unusual exhibit the girls had ever seen. Enlarged glass eyes hung on all the walls. In display cases beneath them were pictures of fish, animals, and humans, with descriptions of their types of eyes.

"Look!" said George. "This caption says a housefly has a compound eye with four thousand lenses."

"No wonder he's hard to catch," Nancy remarked.

Just then all the lights went out. The room was in complete darkness, but in a moment a reddish light began to appear high on the rear wall.

Seconds later it became a fiery, glowing eye!

CHAPTER IV

Fiery Red Hair

FOR several seconds Nancy, Bess, and George stood transfixed by the awesome sight of the glowing eye. At times it blinked and seemed to grow redder.

Bess grabbed Nancy's hand. "What is it?" she whispered tensely.

"I don't know."

"Let's get out of here," Bess pleaded. "This place gives me the creeps."

"Not yet," Nancy answered. "I want to see what happens."

The words were barely said when the glowing eye disappeared. There was pitch blackness for several seconds, then the ceiling lights came on. Nancy turned to ask Miss Wilkin for an explanation.

She had vanished!

"Where did she go and why?" George asked. "She's a strange person."

Bess and George started for the entrance, but Nancy paused to look closely at the spot where the glowing eye had appeared. Though the wall was of wood and paneled in large squares, there was no visible opening or sliding section near the glowing eye. Nancy found a high stool and set it under the panel where the glowing eye had shone. She stood on the stool but was unable to move the panel. And the wood was not hot!

Nancy was sure no image of the eye had been projected onto the wall.

"There must be a cold light behind this panel," she said to herself. "A very bright heatless light."

Her friends had come back. "Learn anything?" George asked.

"No," Nancy replied. "It's a puzzle."

The girls found Miss Wilkin at her desk in the entrance hall. She still had the same expressionless look and offered no explanation of what had happened. Nancy asked her for one.

The woman answered stiffly, "I left to see why the lights went out."

"And the glowing eye?" Nancy prodded.

"That," Miss Wilkin replied, "is used by the engineering students at Emerson who come here to attend lectures given by our member scientists."

"And are the students supposed to give an explanation of the glowing eye?" Nancy asked.

"Yes, but so far none of them has."

The woman stood up and escorted the visitors to the front door. She seemed eager to have them leave.

Nancy smiled and said, "May we come again sometime and see more of the exhibits?"

"If you wish," Miss Wilkin replied, but there was no cordiality in her voice.

The girls drove off, discussing the strange adventure.

"Do you suppose," George asked, "that Ned is connected with this glowing eye bit?"

"Perhaps," Nancy replied. "He's in the engineering school. But I'm surprised that he didn't mention it when I told him about the glowing eye."

"I'm not." George smiled. "Maybe he thought he could find a solution on his own," she teased.

Nancy said, "Ned may have figured out the secret of the glowing eye and been kidnapped because of his discovery."

"That could connect the kidnappers with the Anderson Museum," George commented.

"Maybe in a roundabout way," Nancy replied. To herself she was saying, "I wonder how much Marty King knows about this."

Bess, silent until now, said, "I didn't like that Miss Wilkin and I wouldn't trust her the length of this car. She's spooky and I'll bet she knows a lot more than she's telling."

"I'm inclined to agree," said Nancy. "Let's stop at the library and see what we can find out about the Anderson Museum."

The girl at the reference desk there told them she had never been to the museum but understood it was a spooky place. "But look in the newspaper file. I think there's an article in one of the papers."

Nancy's search was not particularly rewarding. She learned that a large fund had been left to the museum as an endowment to take care of it for educational purposes. There was no mention of a glowing eye.

"Perhaps Burt and Dave will know something about it," George suggested.

Nancy drove directly to the Omega Chi Epsilon fraternity house. Burt and Dave had just come in and greeted the girls warmly. Burt was a rather stocky, athletic blond boy; Dave was slender and blond. They played on the college football team with Ned.

"Any news of Ned?" Nancy asked immediately.

"Not a word," Burt replied. "But Dave and I tracked down a bit of information that might link a certain man with Ned's disappearance."

"Tell me about him," Nancy begged.

Burt said that in one of Ned's engineering courses there was a graduate student with fiery red hair who worked next to Ned in the lab. "He disappeared at the same time Ned did."

"We also learned," Dave added, "that this Zapp Crosson had his pilot's license."

Nancy was intrigued by this information. "So he could have flown the mysterious copter and known how to program the craft to fly itself."

The boys nodded and Burt said, "Nancy, we thought you'd probably know what to do next."

"Any clues about where the copter went?" she asked.

Dave said no one in the vicinity of Emerson knew anything about a helicopter which had the same registration number as the pilotless craft. The local police had made inquiries at a small airfield on the outskirts of Emerson, and also talked with members of a balloon club nearby. No one had a lead.

"It's still early enough to do some exploring before dinner," Dave said. "While you girls are in Emerson you can stay here in our first-floor guest room."

Bess giggled. "I didn't know you had one."

Dave grinned. "Oh, old Omega Chi Epsilon aims to keep up to date," he said.

The girls were led to a charming room with three beds in it and an adjoining bath.

"I'll take your car, Nancy, and fill it with gas," Burt offered. "Meet you all in front in ten minutes."

While the girls were washing their hands and combing their hair, George asked Nancy, "What are your thoughts about Zapp Crosson?"

Nancy replied, "I've been wondering if there was any connection between Zapp's project and an experiment on which Ned might have been working. Ned may have been keeping his own a secret until he had completed the experiment."

Just then the boys returned. They knew where the nearby airfields were located, so the five young people climbed into the car. Bess and George told them the story of the glowing eye.

Nancy felt lonesome without Ned, and started worrying even more about him than she had before. Sensing this, Dave said lightly, "Speaking of glowing eyes, I learned in bio class today that a crayfish's eye has four thousand parts. Each one is a separate eye."

George grinned. "I didn't know the bottom of the *sea* had enough to *see* to require that many eyes."

"Oh, George," said her cousin Bess, "that's a horrible pun."

The others laughed. Burt, who was at the wheel, asked, "Where to?"

Nancy smiled. "Directly northeast from my home in River Heights."

"Emerson is slightly northeast," Burt replied, "so suppose we go due east."

Everyone agreed. Within ten minutes they

came to a private flying field. A helicopter was just coming in. Burt turned into the driveway and went directly toward the whirlybird's landing spot.

A pleasant-looking young pilot leaped down. "Hi!" he said. "Want a ride?"

Nancy jumped from the car. "Do you take people sightseeing?" she asked as an idea flashed into her mind.

"Sure thing. Any place within a radius of a hundred and fifty miles. My rates are low."

Nancy thought so too when she heard what they were.

"How many passengers can you take?"

"Three."

"We'll go," Nancy said. "Are you ready?"

"In a few minutes. I'll fill 'er up with fuel, and take you up for an hour."

While the pilot was doing this, Nancy quickly explained to her friends that she thought it was a marvelous opportunity to view the countryside near Emerson. "Which two of you want to go?"

Bess and Dave offered to stay on the ground. "I'd like to look around and see the planes here," Dave said.

Quarter of an hour later the three passengers climbed aboard and the helicopter rose.

"I'm Glenn Munson," the pilot said. "Anything in particular you'd like to see?"

Nancy introduced herself and her friends. "Yes. As many airfields public and private that you have time to show us."

Glenn raised his eyebrows. "For any special reason?"

Nancy told of the mysterious helicopter landing on the Drews' lawn. "Have you ever seen or heard of a robot copter around this area?" she asked.

"Sure. A friend of mine who's a computer expert has one. Want to meet him?"

Nancy was so excited she could hardly keep her voice calm. But she managed to say, "We'd love to."

Munson steered his craft in a half circle, flew a few miles, then descended. "There's Jerry now," he said, "just tuning up his robot copter to take off." Jerry's helicopter was much smaller than the one which had landed on the Drews' front lawn, and Nancy assumed this was the reason the police had not mentioned it.

She and the others jumped down from their craft and were introduced to Jerry Faber, a tall, lanky young man with twinkling eyes.

"Nancy's looking for a certain robot copter," Glenn said.

"One that's larger than yours," she told Faber.

Jerry grinned. "Sorry I can't help you. But come, I'll show you my real beauty of a copter."

He led the group to a barn at one edge of the field and opened the door. Before them stood a big, shiny new helicopter.

"There's Emmy," Jerry said proudly. "She's not a robot but I can take ten passengers in her. And she has a long range—three hundred and fifty miles."

Nancy was disappointed that neither helicopter was the one she had hoped to find, but said, "This big one certainly is beautiful. Do you use it just for pleasure?"

"No, I fly executives of nearby companies on short business trips, and sometimes other people. I had a mysterious passenger a week ago. He didn't even give me his full name. He just said, 'Call me Crossy.' "

"Crossy?" Burt burst out. "What did he look like?"

"Had bright red hair."

"He's the one!" Burt exclaimed. "We think—" A warning look from Nancy kept him from saying, "We think he's a kidnapper."

"Do you know him?" Glenn asked in surprise.

Burt replied that the man in question might be a graduate student at Emerson who had disappeared.

"Where did you fly him?" Nancy inquired.

Jerry thought a moment. "Oh, I remember now. It was over River Heights."

The visitors exchanged glances. Nancy asked

why Jerry thought Crossy was mysterious. She was told that the man took binoculars from his pocket when they reached River Heights and trained them on every house in town.

"I finally laughed and asked him, 'You got a girl friend down there?' He said, 'Sort of. She's a smart one. Knows the law like a lawyer'!"

Nancy started. Could the girl be Marty King? If so, what did she know about Crosson? Was she playing up to him to get information concerning the mystery of the glowing eye?

"Did Crossy tell you anything else?" Nancy asked.

"No. He talked very little, but he did ask me a lot of questions about complicated computer programming."

Burt said the graduate student from Emerson was a whiz in this subject. "If you ever hear from Crossy, or see him, please let us know."

"I sure will," Jerry replied, "and now I must go to keep an appointment. Look around all you like."

The group thanked the pilot and said good-by. Jerry hurried back to his small helicopter and got in. He spun the rotors and took off. The others watched intently.

Suddenly George cried out, "Oh my goodness! Jerry's in trouble!"

Everyone gazed in horror at his whirlybird which was spiraling toward the ground!

CHAPTER V

A Strange Prison

As the group watched Jerry's helicopter, which apparently was out of control, Glenn suddenly began to laugh. The others looked at him in amazement.

"Jerry had me fooled too for a few minutes. He's not in trouble. Jerry's doing some acrobatics for you. Pretty intricate flying maneuvers for a copter. He's really good."

"I'll say he is," Burt spoke up.

Jerry leveled his craft and flew off. Those on the ground could visualize him grinning over his trick. Then they turned and walked back to look again at the helicopter in the hangar. Nancy climbed up to look inside.

"What a battery of gadgets!" she exclaimed. "There must be a hundred push buttons and levers and lights on this instrument panel!"

As her eyes wandered over the intricate setup, Nancy noticed a penny on the floor.

"I wonder if Jerry dropped this," she thought, "or some passenger—perhaps Crosson!"

Nancy picked up the penny and examined it. The coin bore the date 1923 S. *"Mm,* that's old and valuable," she said to herself. "It's like one Dad has. Shall I leave it here?"

She decided to ask Glenn to return it to Jerry. Nancy stepped down and handed the penny to their pilot. She made her request, then added, "If Jerry knows who dropped it, please call me." She wrote down the telephone number of the fraternity house.

Glenn promised that he would and said they had better leave. "I have another job in half an hour," he explained.

The pilot took his passengers back to the airfield, then hurried off. Nancy's car was not in sight.

"Bess and Dave must have taken it," Nancy remarked.

The couple had driven off in the convertible soon after their friends had left.

"Let's do some sleuthing in this area," Dave suggested as they headed for the road.

"Where do we start?" Bess asked. "This is farming country. I'm getting one of Nancy's hunches that Zapp Crosson or whoever kidnapped Ned would pick a secluded section like this one to hide out."

"Right."

After traveling a few miles they came to an old, dilapidated two-story farmhouse. Bess went up on the porch of rotting floorboards. The windows had no curtains and she could see there were only a few pieces of half-broken furniture inside the house.

"I guess no one lives here," she called out to Dave.

He hopped from the car and came to take a look. "I wonder if the house is locked." Dave tried the front door. It opened without a key.

"Let's explore," he urged.

"No thanks," said Bess. "Deserted houses with unlocked doors aren't my idea of safe places to investigate."

Dave made no comment and walked in. "If I don't return in thirty minutes, get the police," he teased, tossing Bess the car keys.

"Oh, I'll come," she decided. Bess was fearful but did not want Dave to think her a coward.

There was a narrow center hall with a steep stairway. A room opened onto it from either side. The rear of the hallway led into the kitchen, which was stocked with canned food. A knife, fork, and spoon lay in the sink alongside an unwashed plate.

"Someone's probably camping out here," Dave remarked.

"And I'll bet," Bess replied, "it's someone who

has no business here. But I don't want to be caught trespassing. Let's go!"

"No," said Dave. "I'd like to find out who the intruder is. I'm going upstairs. You stay here on guard."

Bess felt uncomfortable being left alone but knew she would be more ill at ease on the floor above. She closed the front door and posted herself near it, but presently began to walk from window to window.

Suddenly she jumped in fright as something heavy fell overhead. Bess rushed to the stairway and called up.

"Dave! Are you all right?"

There was no answer. Putting her fears aside, Bess vaulted up the steps two at a time, all the while calling Dave's name. He did not reply. She hurried through the scantily furnished bedrooms but found no sign of her friend. She could not figure out what had fallen. There was no stairway to a third floor.

"Oh, Dave, where are you?" Bess wailed.

She began opening one closet door after another, each time with a shudder as to what she might find. Finally Bess reached the last closet. As she opened the door she could hear muffled sounds. Nobody was inside. Bess stepped forward to put her ear to the wall.

"O-o-oh!" Bess exclaimed as the floor suddenly opened and she plummeted downward.

The startled girl landed in the pitch darkness on something soft. It moved under her. She heard a groan.

"Dave!" Bess murmured. "Oh, I must have hurt you!"

"You sure knocked the wind out of me. Good thing I'm used to tackle football!"

"Where are we?" Bess asked.

"At the bottom of a clothes chute," Dave answered. "It was lucky there were some things in it to cushion my fall."

Bess asked how they were going to escape. "Besides, I don't want to get caught by that person who comes here. He might be dangerous."

Dave admitted he had not yet found an opening, but was sure there was one.

The two captives felt every inch of the wall and floor of their prison. When they could find no doorknob nor a bolt, they began to push and press the wood.

"I'm sure of one thing," said Dave. "We're below the first floor in a cellar. There *must* be an opening in this wooden chute."

"*Sh!*" Bess whispered as he finished. "Listen!"

She had heard the front door slam. Now there were footsteps overhead.

Bess clung to Dave's arm. "We'll be found!" she whispered tensely.

"In here? I doubt it," he said, trying to reassure her with a little hug.

The two waited in silence. Floorboards creaked as the heavy stepping person trudged all through the house. Bess and Dave assumed he had spotted the car in front and had come to investigate. Evidently satisfied the place was vacant, the man slammed the front door again. In a few moments Bess and Dave heard an automobile drive off.

"Probably a policeman," Dave suggested. "At first I thought he might be the person who's using this place."

Once more he and Bess began to push on the walls of the clothes chute. Finally Dave put his finger in a small knothole and was able to move a concealed door to one side. The couple stepped out into a cellar dimly lighted by the sun streaming through a small window. The place was empty except for two musty washtubs and a stack of dusty newspapers.

"How do we get out of this prison?" Bess asked Dave, after glancing around. No door or other exit was visible.

While she searched for a hidden exit in a wall, Dave's eyes roved back and forth across the ceiling. It was thick with dirt and cobwebs, but he thought he could detect a movable section under the kitchen. He mentioned his discovery to Bess.

"Climb up to my shoulders and try to open this," Dave said. "The people who lived here must have used a ladder."

Dave leaned over. Bess pulled herself onto his

shoulders and stood up. She quickly found that a section of the ceiling could be pushed upward. With a little effort Bess eased herself through.

"How are you going to get out?" she asked Dave.

"Don't worry. The first thing I want to do is examine these clothes in the chute. There might be a clue for Nancy to work on."

Bess quickly looked for a stepladder and found one in a closet.

Dave reported with a laugh, "All men's clothes in the chute and nothing in them but a penny in a shirt pocket."

Bess giggled. "Bring it up here. Might be a good-luck penny. Here's a ladder. I'll hand it to you."

Dave took it and in a moment he was beside Bess. Then he reached down and pulled up the ladder.

"We'd better go," Bess said. "Nancy and George and Burt may be back and wondering where we went."

The two hurried outside without meeting anyone and drove back to the airfield. Their friends were waiting.

"Where have you been?" George said petulantly. "We thought you'd been kidnapped too."

Dave replied, "We were prisoners. It's lucky we got back here. Bess, shall we tell them where

"Try to open it," Dave said.

we were being held?" There was a twinkle in his eye.

Bess smiled. "After they tell us where they went."

Nancy knew there was no use coaxing, so she briefed the couple on the helicopter trip, and mentioned the 1923 S penny she had found in Jerry Faber's big copter.

"I found a penny also," said Dave. He took the coin out of a pocket in his jeans. After looking at the date on it, he exclaimed, "This is a 1923 S penny too!"

CHAPTER VI

Mysterious Burglary

FINALLY Nancy said, "I have a hunch that Zapp Crosson owns both pennies." After hearing Bess and Dave's story, she said, "He could have dropped the first one in the copter on his trip to look over River Heights, and left the other one at the farmhouse."

George spoke up. "In other words, you think he put the second penny in the pocket of his shirt and then changed clothes."

Nancy told her she thought Crosson had done more than this. "I believe the farmhouse is a hideout for him."

Bess was sure the suspect was not carrying on any kind of experiments at the house. "Dave and I looked over the place thoroughly and didn't find anything unusual until we fell down the clothes chute."

George laughed. "I'll bet he doesn't go there just to wash his clothes."

Burt said, "More likely he goes there to put on a disguise of some kind to fool the police. For one thing, he'd want to cover that fiery red hair of his."

There was a great deal of discussion among the young people as Burt drove along. Nancy said she thought the farmhouse should be guarded. "But I don't like to notify the police until we know for sure that Crosson is our man."

Dave said he had a suggestion. "How about Burt and me staying at the house for the night? I saw plenty of canned food. If there's no car around, Crosson won't suspect anyone is there. When he comes in, we'll give him a football rush before he can escape."

Burt turned the car and headed toward the farmhouse. When they had almost reached it, he said, "You girls go on back to Emerson and pick us up at the farm early in the morning."

They agreed. Half a mile from the house the two boys got out and to keep from being seen approached the building from the rear.

Meanwhile, Nancy had taken the wheel and the girls had gone on. When they returned to the fraternity house, students crowded around and asked many questions.

"Any news of Ned?"

"What did you find out?"

The girls admitted that they had learned very little but suspected a certain place might offer a clue, so Burt and Dave were spending the night there to see what they could find out. This seemed to satisfy the boys, and the girls hurried off to the guest room.

"I certainly need a bath and a shampoo," Bess spoke up. "Anybody mind if I use the shower first?"

"Go ahead," said Nancy. She sat down in a chair and stared out a window, but her mind was not on the scenery. She was recalling the day's adventures and trying to fit the pieces of the puzzle together. She asked herself, "If Crosson goes to the farmhouse, does he bring Ned with him?

"Probably not," the young detective decided. "Oh, Ned, where are you?" she thought wistfully. "If you can't send me another message, concentrate real hard on transmitting a clue into this brain of mine."

A while later George tapped her on the shoulder. "Time's up for daydreaming," she said. "Bathroom's free. Your turn for a shower."

Almost absentmindedly Nancy got up and went to take a refreshing bath. After it, she felt less edgy and hurried to put on fresh clothes for dinner.

Ned's fraternity brothers were very kind and solicitous and tried their best to entertain the three girls, Nancy in particular. When dinner was over, a tall blond boy with deep-blue eyes, named Tom Rankin, put some hit records on the stereo. Nancy enjoyed the music, but before one album had finished, she was called to the telephone.

"Hello! Who is this?" she asked.

"Never mind who I am. What I want to know is, where are Burt Eddleton and Dave Evans?"

Nancy was instantly alert. Instead of giving the information, she said, "I won't answer your question until you identify yourself."

She waited for an answer but none came. There were several seconds of silence, then the caller hung up.

As Nancy came back to join the group, she began to worry about Burt and Dave. She asked the boy who had originally taken the call if the speaker had asked for either Burt or Dave.

"Yes, he did. When I said they were not here, he wanted to speak to you. Is something wrong?"

"I don't know, but the man wouldn't give me his name," Nancy replied.

Bess and George were upset when they heard what had happened. Bess, who was frantic with worry, said, "I'm sure the caller was Crosson. He isn't satisfied with having kidnapped Ned. Now he's going to get Dave and Burt!"

George did not share her cousin's fears. "I'm sure Burt and Dave will know how to take care of themselves if he arrives."

"But suppose," said Bess, "that he brings along some pals and they overpower Dave and Burt?"

There was a discussion about whether or not the girls should notify the police, but they had confidence in their friends' resourcefulness and strength to meet any emergency.

George said, "Let's get some sleep and go out there early in the morning."

The girls said good night to Ned's fraternity brothers and went to bed. None of them slept well and were up at six o'clock.

The friendly blond boy Tom Rankin was also up. It was his turn to be on kitchen duty. Nancy, Bess, and George helped him and the four had breakfast together.

"Where are you off to?" he asked.

"To get Burt and Dave," Nancy replied, but gave no other information.

When the girls reached the farmhouse, it appeared to be deserted. Nancy opened the front door and called out. There was no answer. Quickly the three made a search of the place and George even got the ladder from the closet and went to the cellar. She looked in the clothes chute. Burt and Dave were not on the premises.

Moments later Nancy, Bess, and George stood in the middle of the living room, staring at one another, the same thought going through their minds. Had Burt and Dave been kidnapped?

"Oh, I can't stand it!" Bess wailed, tears welling up in her eyes. "Why did we ever let the boys stay here?"

"Shush!" George commanded. "Crying over the situation isn't helping any. Put on your thinking cap, Bess, and help us figure out—"

Nancy interrupted to ask a pertinent question. "George, were there clothes in the chute?"

George admitted that she had not noticed. Once more she climbed down the ladder to the cellar, then slid back the door to the chute. There was nothing in it.

"Now I know Crosson was here!" she thought.

George was not the kind of girl to give in to tears, but it was difficult for her to come back up the ladder and tell the others of her suspicion.

"I'm going outside and look around," she said.

Nancy and Bess began to hunt in the house for anything which might give them a clue to the boys' whereabouts. They hoped that Burt and Dave might have managed to leave some kind of message. But their search revealed no leads.

George, who had just finished scrutinizing the ground in front of the farmhouse for clues, saw a State Police patrol car coming. She was about to hail it, when the car pulled in and stopped. The uniformed driver opened the door on the passenger side and shouted to George, "Is Nancy Drew here?"

"Yes, she is," George replied, wondering whether the man was bringing bad news.

George rushed up to the front door and called

to Nancy. She came downstairs with Bess at her heels.

"I'm Anthony Russo," the policeman said.

The girls introduced themselves and Nancy said, "Do you have a message for me?"

The officer nodded and said that he had been there earlier and talked to Burt and Dave who had explained their reason for trespassing. The officer grinned. "I found out they hadn't had a meal since lunchtime yesterday so I took them to Campbell's Diner in town. You're to meet them there."

The three girls heaved sighs of relief and Nancy told the policeman how frightened they had been that possibly the boys had been kidnapped.

Russo laughed. "It would be pretty hard to subdue those two huskies," he said.

Nancy asked the officer if he knew who lived at the farmhouse.

"Nobody."

"Do you think a tramp might be using the place?" Nancy queried.

Russo said he doubted this, although he had noticed a dirty dish and silverware in the sink. "I come by here fairly often and I've never yet seen anybody around."

Nancy thanked him for bringing the message and said the girls would pick up the boys at once.

When they arrived at the diner, Burt and Dave were standing in front. "Hi!" they said cheerily.

Bess did not smile in return. "Why didn't you leave us a note?" she scolded. "We've been beside ourselves with worry that you had been kidnapped."

"Kidnapped!" Burt said, and burst into laughter.

He told them that the boys had found nothing at the farmhouse to connect Crosson with the place and had not been disturbed during the night.

George was unwilling to accept this statement without an explanation. "When did the clothes vanish from the chute?" she asked.

Burt and Dave looked blank. They admitted they had failed to look in the chute and had no idea when the clothes might have been taken out.

"But I'm sure it wasn't after we arrived," Burt declared. "Someone must have removed them between the time Bess and Dave were there and we guys went back to the farmhouse."

On their return trip to Emerson, Bess and George continued to tease Dave and Burt. They accused them of sleeping so soundly that they did not hear the man, and worst of all of snoring so loudly that the man knew the boys were there.

"Enough! Enough!" Dave cried out, putting his hands over his ears. "I have to concentrate now on my next class." He looked at his watch.

"Burt," he said, "you'd better speed up or we'll both be late."

Nearing the campus, Nancy told the boys about the mysterious phone call asking where they were. "I wonder if it was before or after the caller visited the farmhouse."

Burt and Dave felt sure it was before. "On the other hand, if he came there after we arrived, he probably didn't realize we were there," Burt added. "We don't snore!"

He drove directly to the classroom building and the boys got out. Nancy took the wheel and headed for the fraternity house. A student was on duty in the front hall.

"Any word about Ned yet?" Nancy asked him.

"Nothing," he answered. "But say, there's been some more excitement on the campus. A burglary!"

"Really?" George spoke up. "Where?"

"Over in the office and lab where the electronic and computer work is done. Ned and Mr. Crosson experimented there. Lots of things were taken."

At once Nancy, Bess, and George wanted to know the full story of the theft. They jumped into the convertible and Nancy sped to the scene. Could there be any connection between the burglary and the mysterious disappearance of Crosson and Ned? Nancy wondered.

CHAPTER VII

The Explosion

WHEN Nancy, Bess, and George reached the laboratory, they found the entrance door wide open. Professor Titus, who was in charge of the department, and a policeman were at work hunting for clues to the burglar's identity. The officer was taking pictures of fingerprints.

Nancy introduced herself and her friends and told the professor that they were trying to solve the mystery of Ned Nickerson's strange disappearance.

"Oh yes," Titus said, "and I understand you are being very thorough. No doubt that is why you are here."

"We've been away on a sleuthing mission and just got back," Nancy explained. "When we learned what had happened here, we came right over."

Professor Titus took the girls to meet the fingerprint expert, who by this time had developed all his pictures from the fast-processing film.

He remarked, "These very faint old ones and the newly made group are the same."

"Does that mean," Nancy asked, "that the person responsible for the theft is well acquainted with this lab?"

The officer was inclined to think so. "I'll see if the college has the fingerprints of everyone using this laboratory."

Professor Titus spoke up. "That has never been required," he said. "I am afraid you'll have to look elsewhere for identification."

Nancy was sorry to hear this. She wanted to mention Crosson's name because in her own mind she felt sure that he had burglarized the lab. But on the other hand, why would he rob the place when he could work there? She decided to say nothing yet to the police.

"Perhaps Crosson has gone away for good," the young detective said to herself.

She asked Professor Titus if it would be all right for her to look around.

"Yes, indeed," he said.

The three girls walked about slowly, examining the long worktables, some with sinks, others with electric outlets. Against one wall were computers of various sizes. The electronic equipment seemed complicated.

"This place is like a maze," she thought.

Idly Nancy wandered over to a metal file cabinet which stood by itself on one side of the room. "I think I'll just peek inside. Maybe I can pick up some information to help solve this case."

She pulled open the top drawer and found it filled with books. They were of a technical and specialized nature and Nancy doubted that they would lend a clue.

"I'll look at them later," she decided, closing the drawer.

Next she drew out the large second drawer. Before Nancy had a chance to find out what it contained, there was a sudden explosion inside the drawer. It tore the file cabinet apart.

The force knocked Nancy against the opposite wall, but fortunately she was not hit by any of the flying debris. The others in the room rushed over to see if she was all right.

"Nancy!" Bess cried out.

"I'm okay," the stunned girl answered shakily. "I must have triggered off a bomb."

As George glanced toward the wreck, she yelled, "Fire! The papers are on fire!"

Professor Titus had rushed to a nearby extinguisher and told the others to get another from the outer office. The flaming papers crackled and sent up greenish smoke. The two extinguishers failed to douse the flames.

"Notify the fire department!" Professor Titus

shouted, and George dashed to the office phone to put in the call.

The odor from the burning contents of the cabinet became intolerable. Everyone was forced to leave and the door was closed. Professor Titus suddenly recalled that there was a manual sprinkler system in the ceiling of the lab. He turned two metal wheels on the wall, then opened the lab door a crack and peered in. Water was streaming down. By the time the firemen arrived, the blaze had been extinguished.

"I guess our equipment isn't needed," said one of the men with a smile, "but we'll investigate the cause of the fire."

Professor Titus looked a little sheepish. "I only remembered about the overhead sprinkler system after we called you," he said. "What I think we do need here is an inspection by the police bomb squad." He told about the explosion in the file cabinet, and the fire captain in charge telephoned at once to the head of the bomb squad.

Nancy remarked to the other girls, "If there was anything important in the file, it's no good to us now."

George replied, "I guess that's the way the burglar planned it."

Nancy turned to Professor Titus. "Please tell me all you know about Zapp Crosson."

"Actually I know very little," he replied. "Why? Do you—?" When the young detective did not offer to explain her interest in the graduate student, Professor Titus went on, "The young man was secretive and uncommunicative. Several times I tried to engage him in conversation, but all he ever told me was that his parents were foreign and he had had part of his education in Europe."

Nancy said she understood that Crosson worked next to Ned in the lab.

"Yes," Professor Titus said, "and he often assisted Ned, mostly when no regular classes were being held in the lab or when no other students were working there on experiments."

At once Nancy thought, "Here's a clue!" She wondered if Ned was doing original experiments. Was Crosson helping him or only being an inquisitive bystander?

At that moment two fully equipped representatives from the police bomb squad arrived. They entered the soaking wet lab and checked every inch of its walls and floor to be sure that no other bombs had been planted.

By this time the rank odor which had accompanied the fire had vanished up the ventilator and the fire captain declared the room was now safe to enter.

"I'd like to take a look around the place again," Nancy told the professor.

"Go ahead," he said. He introduced her to the bomb squad men and said she was an amateur detective. "But her methods seem very professional," he added with a smile.

"Then we would be glad for any help you can give us," one member of the squad said. "I'm Jake Reilly."

Nancy grinned. "Thank you for the compliment," she said. "I'm sure I can't tell you well-trained men anything you wouldn't be able to find out yourselves."

Professor Titus spoke up quickly. With a grin he said, "The police have not yet found our students Ned Nickerson and Zapp Crosson. Miss Drew, on the other hand, has uncovered several leads."

The men were very much interested. "Can you tell us about any of them?" Reilly asked the young detective.

Nancy took a deep breath before answering. "I'm afraid Professor Titus is exaggerating about my discoveries. I became involved in the case because of a strangely worded message I received in a robot copter. Actually it was a warning to me to beware of Cyclops."

"Cyclops?" Reilly repeated. "What is that?"

"That's what I'm trying to find out," Nancy revealed.

She changed the subject so that she would not be questioned any further. "I'd like to continue what I was doing before the explosion, if it's all right."

"Go ahead," Reilly replied.

Nancy walked off, scanning the littered floor. Suddenly in one corner she noticed a giant-sized glass eye. Her heart pounding with excitement, she hurried toward it. The object might be a link to the intriguing eye at the Anderson Museum! Although this eye was not glowing, she asked Reilly if it had been tested for radioactivity.

"It has none," he reported.

Nancy picked up the glass eye. Upon close inspection she discovered that the glass was a lid over a painted eye. She lifted the lid and studied the eye. Was it hiding something beneath? A small computer perhaps? She gazed at it a long time, then closed the lid.

"Professor Titus, do you know anything about this?" Nancy asked.

"Never saw it before."

"How about the glowing eye at the Anderson Museum?" the young detective queried.

"I don't know anything about it."

Nancy thought this was strange since she had been told the eye belonged to Emerson's science department, and students from there were in charge of it.

Suddenly the eye began to quiver in Nancy's hand. The catch had become unfastened. Before she could close it, a voice from inside the gadget said, "Don't touch me! I am the deadly Cyclops!"

The young detective quickly closed the lid and

laid the eye back on the floor. The voice stopped speaking.

"Let me see it," Reilly said in bewilderment.

Nancy handed it to him and in a few seconds the message was repeated. Reilly closed the lid and the voice stopped.

"This will bear closer investigation," he said. "I'll take it along. I don't quite trust the mechanism inside. Possibly it could trigger another explosion—if the person handling it does not obey. Girls, you'd better leave the lab at once to avoid any further danger! Hurry!"

CHAPTER VIII

Puzzling Package

THE three girls returned to the fraternity house. It was nearly lunchtime and Burt and Dave had come in.

"Well, how did the three detectives make out this morning?" Burt asked. "Did you uncover Cyclops?"

"No, but we heard from him," George replied with a mysterious air.

"What!" Dave exclaimed.

Little by little the events of the morning in the lab were unfolded. Burt and Dave stared in astonishment.

"A bomb explosion!" Burt gasped. "You're lucky you weren't injured. So you think maybe Crosson was hiding something that he didn't want anybody to see. What could it have been?"

Nancy said, "Plans and perhaps drawings for some experiment on which he was working." Suddenly she stopped speaking and stared into space.

Then she went on, "I suspect that Crosson was trying to learn something from Ned, which I'm sure he wouldn't reveal, so Crosson either stole it or was trying to. That file cabinet may even have contained some of Ned's work that Crosson didn't know about. It would be a shame if it's ruined."

The conversation was interrupted by a student who said there was a telephone call for Nancy Drew. She went off to answer it and found that an agent from the FBI was on the line.

"The police asked the Bureau to keep you advised of any new developments concerning Ned Nickerson," the man said. "I regret that so far we have no trace of either him or Zapp Crosson."

"I'm sorry to hear that," Nancy replied. "My friends and I haven't had any luck either, but we're continuing our search."

The agent said that two FBI men were coming to investigate Ned's college room. "We'll be there in about two hours. Will you try to meet us at the fraternity house?"

Nancy said she would be glad to and was looking forward to the men's report.

In the meantime she and her friends had lunch. Burt and Dave had to leave directly afterward to attend more lectures.

"Will it be all right for Bess and George and me to go to Ned's room to watch the FBI men work?" Nancy asked the boys.

Burt grinned. "If the agents have no objection, I don't see any reason why you shouldn't watch. But be sure you ask for identification when the men arrive. We don't want any impostors going through Ned's personal belongings."

Nancy nodded, then smiled. "Maybe by tonight we'll have another surprise for you."

The boys went off. Soon two men came to the house and asked for Nancy. After they had shown identification, she led them upstairs. George and Bess followed.

A sudden wave of panic came over Nancy. Would Ned ever return to this room?

"He absolutely must," she said to herself.

The FBI agents were very thorough. They searched every inch of the room. Finally one of the men began to open the desk drawers. He called the girls' attention to the fact that there was nothing in them.

"That's unusual for a college student," he remarked.

George spoke up. "Maybe Ned removed the papers."

"But why?" Bess asked.

The agent looked up at Nancy. "Perhaps Miss Drew has an answer."

"I can make a guess," Nancy replied. "Did you know that there had been a burglary in one of the labs? A great deal of equipment was taken. Isn't it possible the same burglar came here to steal some science papers that belonged to Ned?"

"Very good reasoning," the agent said. Then he picked up a small paper which had lain upside down in the drawer. "This is the only thing in here, but it looks interesting," he added, turning it right side up. He handled it carefully so as not to smudge any fingerprints that might be on it.

The others peered over his shoulder. Someone had drawn a sketch of an oversized eye. Under it were the letters ΚΥΚΛΟΨ.

Everyone stared at the paper and Bess murmured, "That awful eye again!"

The agent turned to his companion. "Do you know what this says?"

"Yes," the other man replied. "It's Greek. I studied Greek at school. These letters spell the word Cyclops."

Hearing this, Bess gave another little cry. "That's the second time today we've come across Cyclops," she told the agents.

Nancy informed the men that Ned Nickerson had not studied Greek so she was inclined to think that someone else had made the drawing.

Everyone started conjecturing about who had left it. The burglar? Another student? A professor? Nancy, however, was convinced that Crosson had given it to Ned or placed it in his room as a warning.

No one had any answers to the questions and the FBI agents admitted there was nothing else in the room to supply a clue. "We'll take this paper along," one of them said, "and have the fingerprints on it analyzed."

The group went downstairs and in a few minutes the agents said good-by. They promised to communicate with Nancy if anything of importance came of their tests.

The three girls returned to the guest room and sat down to talk. "It seems to me," said Bess, "that things are getting to be more of a mess instead of being straightened out."

Nancy agreed but George came to her friend's defense. "I think Nancy has accomplished a great deal. She has practically proved that Ned was kidnapped and probably by Crosson who was afraid of having an undergraduate receive more praise for some experiment than he would for one of his."

"You could be right," Bess remarked. "But where do we go from here?"

At that moment the extension phone in their room rang. Nancy answered. A student who had taken the call said that Ned Nickerson's mother was on the wire.

"She has something very important to tell you, Nancy," he said.

"Thank you," she replied to the boy, and he transferred the call to her phone.

"Nancy dear, is this you?"

"Yes, Mrs. Nickerson. How are you?"

"Oh, I'm all right, but worried of course."

"I understand you have some important news for me."

Ned's mother said she felt sure it was important and went on to say that a large package had arrived from Emerson. It was from Ned and had been mailed to her and Mr. Nickerson several days before.

"We can't understand why Ned sent those things home during the term. Surely he would need them for his college work."

Nancy asked what was in the package.

"It was filled with papers and all kinds of technical drawings from science courses."

"Mrs. Nickerson," said Nancy, "was there a drawing of an eye?"

"No, dear. Why do you ask?"

Nancy said that she thought Ned might be interested in an experiment to do with a glowing eye, then asked, "Does the word Cyclops appear anywhere among the papers?"

"No. That's derived from Greek, isn't it?" Mrs. Nickerson inquired. "Nothing in the contents contains a Greek word."

She went on to say that no letter of explanation had come.

"What kind of drawings are they?" Nancy queried.

"Oh, various geometrical figures, but one thing we did notice. There were several sketches of helicopters. My husband and I don't know anything about helicopters so I can't tell you what type they are. Do you think Ned was taking flying lessons?"

"I never heard him mention it," Nancy replied, then inquired if there were any charts for computer programming.

"I have no idea," Ned's mother replied. "I wouldn't know one if I saw it!"

Nancy asked a few more questions about the papers, but Mrs. Nickerson could not answer them. Suddenly she suggested, "How about you and Bess and George coming here for a little visit and going through Ned's papers? You might even find a message from him hidden among them!"

"Oh, thank you very much," Nancy replied. "When would you like us to come?"

Mrs. Nickerson said, "The sooner the better. Can you start right away?"

"I don't see any reason why not," Nancy replied. "Would you hold the line a minute while I ask Bess and George?"

Nancy turned and quickly relayed the message. They agreed at once to go.

As the girls packed their bags and wrote a note to Burt and Dave, they discussed what Nancy had learned from Mrs. Nickerson.

"I can't understand," said Bess, "why Ned bothered to send all those papers home."

George had an answer. "Perhaps he suspected

he might be kidnapped and wanted to keep the papers safe. Or it's just possible he decided to vanish so he couldn't be kidnapped."

Nancy thought this over. Presently she said, "If Ned did go away for a personal reason, maybe he's doing some detective work on his own."

George nodded. "True. And where does Crosson fit in? Is Ned trailing him because he suspects him of something dishonest?"

Bess sighed. "It's all so complicated. But I don't think Ned disappeared voluntarily."

In a few minutes the girls were ready to leave. Nancy decided to call Hannah Gruen and tell her about the change in plans and ask her to notify the Marvins and Faynes. She dialed the number. There was a long wait before her ringing was answered. To her surprise it was not Hannah's voice that said hello. Instead it was Marty King's!

CHAPTER IX

The Spy

THERE was a soft laugh at the other end of the line. "I guess you're surprised to find me at your house," Marty said.

"A little," Nancy replied, trying not to let her voice betray how startled she was. "I suppose you're there to help Dad with some specific kind of work."

Marty King giggled. "Work, yes, but not legal work."

Nancy's heart began to beat a little faster. What did Mr. Drew's assistant mean by that remark? Did she mean detective work?

Marty went on to explain. "Your father is out of town and I didn't know where to reach him. Mrs. Gruen, your housekeeper, telephoned me to give a message to your dad. A close relative of hers was taken ill and she had to leave immediately. She would not be able to get dinner for Mr. Drew."

"I see," said Nancy.

Marty King informed the young detective that she was an excellent cook and thought it would be fun to surprise the lawyer with a good meal.

"I'm planning to make an unusual French dish," she added.

"I'm sure my father will enjoy it," Nancy said without enthusiasm.

Marty asked if there was any message Nancy wished her to give Mr. Drew.

"Yes," the young detective replied. "Please tell him that Bess, George, and I are leaving Emerson to go to Ned Nickerson's home and stay overnight. By the way, Marty, how are you making out with the glowing eye case?" Nancy asked her. "Solved it yet?"

Marty was taken off guard. She stammered a moment, then finally said, "My key contact has disappeared."

"That's too bad," Nancy said, but secretly was relieved to hear it. Without her contact, Marty could not work on the case which Nancy considered to be hers!

"By the way," said Marty, "any news of Ned?"

"Nothing concrete," Nancy replied evasively. Recalling what Jerry Faber had told her about the conversation with his mysterious passenger, she wondered if Zapp Crosson had been

Marty King's source of information. She asked, "Marty, was your key contact a special friend?"

The young lawyer giggled. "He'd like to be—" There was a long pause, then she continued, "There's someone else I like much better."

Nancy's mind was racing with ideas. Could Marty possibly mean her father? Before Nancy could think of a way to induce Marty to tell her, the other girl abruptly changed the subject.

"I have something cooking, so I must get back to it. I'll give your father the message. Bye now."

Nancy put down the phone and at once Bess said, "Don't keep us in suspense. What is Marty King doing at your house?"

Nancy smiled. "Getting my father's dinner ready. Hannah is away."

"Ah-ah," said Bess with a wink at George—a wink that Nancy did not fail to see.

Her cousin was about to continue the teasing but changed her mind. A woebegone look had come over Nancy's face and George decided to drop the subject.

"We'd better get going," she said. "It's a fairly long ride to Mapleton."

Nancy nodded. The girls picked up their bags and light coats and went out to the car. There was little traffic and the drive did not take as long as they had expected. They arrived at the Nickerson home about five o'clock.

Ned's mother greeted them at the front door.

She was pretty and dressed attractively. Bess gazed enviously at the woman's slender figure.

Mr. Nickerson was at home also. He and Ned closely resembled each other, and the youthful-looking older man was still athletic like his son.

"I certainly hope you girls can solve this mystery soon," he said. "Naturally, Mrs. Nickerson and I are extremely worried. We know Ned can usually take care of himself, but if he is being held by someone who has no scruples, he may be in great danger."

George remarked, "A break in the case should come soon. We have some good leads and I hope Nancy can find another one among the papers Ned sent home."

The girls were taken upstairs to two bedrooms. As soon as they had put down their luggage, Nancy said, "I can't wait to see the papers. May I look at them now?"

"They're still in Ned's room," Mrs. Nickerson replied. "As soon as you freshen up, I'll meet you in there and show them to you."

Within five minutes Nancy was looking at the drawings, figures, and exposition in the various science papers Ned had written.

"They are very technical," she remarked to Mrs. Nickerson. "I'm sure, though, that they are not for a computer."

Ned's mother watched Nancy work for a while, then excused herself.

"Before you go," said Nancy, "tell me, have you a large blackboard?"

Mrs. Nickerson said there was one in Ned's closet. "And I think there's chalk in the desk. Why do you want the board, dear?"

Nancy said she had become fascinated by a set of numbers arranged in a pattern on one of the papers. "From a distance they seemed to be the outline of an eye. I want to copy them."

She said she wondered if Ned had discovered the formula for a cold light glowing eye. "The numbers may be a code—a code that Zapp Crosson wanted desperately to get!"

"I know how interested you are in working on the case," Ned's mother said. "But we must eat. I didn't feel like cooking, so I arranged for all of us to have dinner at Flannery's restaurant. Do you mind if we go ahead, Nancy, so that we won't lose our reservation?"

"Please do," Nancy replied. "What I want to work on shouldn't take long. I'll meet you all there as soon as I can."

Mrs. Nickerson nodded, left the room, and went downstairs. A short time later Nancy heard the group drive off in the Nickerson car.

She went to the closet and brought out the blackboard which opened up and stood on four legs.

With her back to the open window, Nancy began to chalk down the numbers from the sheet

Turning, Nancy caught sight of a man.

on the desk. She decided it would be wiser to memorize them rather than write them on anything to take with her. This way they could not fall into dishonest hands in case the copy was stolen or lost. It did not take her long to sketch the eye-shaped code.

As Nancy stood memorizing the numbers and their position in the eye, she suddenly had a creepy feeling that she was being watched. Turning toward the window Nancy caught sight of a man's head. He had bright red hair!

His face was nearly hidden by his hands which held a sketching pad and pencil. He was copying the numbers that were on the blackboard!

In a flash Nancy laid the blackboard face down on the floor and dashed to the window. The spy had vanished. When she looked down the side of the house, he was just reaching the last rung of a ladder. The man raced for the street.

Nancy ran down the stairs and out the door. She looked for a license plate on the spy's disappearing car. It had none!

"He won't get far before a traffic policeman stops him!" she said to herself. "I'll follow his car."

Quickly Nancy closed the front door of the house and sprinted to her car, parked on the street. She pulled a key from a hiding place and sped after the fleeing red-haired man. The young detective had seen him turn a corner and went that way.

A wild thought came to her. If the man was not stopped by the police, he might lead her to Ned! But by the time she reached the next corner the spy had disappeared. There was no one around for Nancy to ask where he might have gone and in a few minutes she gave up the chase.

Nancy decided she should return to the house. Ned's bedroom window was open and a ladder stood under it. Anyone could enter. Upon reaching the house, Nancy jumped from the car and hurried toward the ladder. Her attention was drawn to a large notebook lying near the bottom rung of the ladder. Could it have been dropped by the man who had started to sketch Ned's code? she wondered.

Nancy walked over and picked up the notebook. Excitedly she opened it.

CHAPTER X

Treacherous Swamp

THE notebook which the stranger had lost was blank except for a single page. On this he had started to copy the numbers from the blackboard. Most of them were there and they had been written in the eye-shaped pattern.

"I wonder if the man who sketched this really was Crosson," Nancy mused. "Maybe he'll return for his notebook," the young detective thought. "I can notify the police to come here and pick him up, if he returns, but I needn't wait for them. The Nickersons are probably already wondering where I am."

Nancy stood deep in thought for a few moments, then she took the pencil attached to the notebook and quickly began to erase the figures. One by one she moved the numbers around so that if they were a code, it certainly was scrambled now! She closed the notebook and laid it back on the ground.

As she did this, another idea came to her. Suppose the spy was the same person who had come to her house and either released or flown the robot copter! If she found the same type of soil on the rungs of the ladder as she had on the copter's tires, it could be a clue. The young detective realized that two days or more had elapsed since the robot copter had taken off from a swampy, wooded area. During that lapse of time mud on shoes could have been scuffed off.

"Or the man might have been wearing different footwear today," she thought.

"I'll take a look, however, to be sure," Nancy decided. "Anyway, since I don't have a key to the house, I'll have to climb the ladder to get back inside and lock all the windows."

Slowly she mounted the rungs, examining each one thoroughly as she went. Every few seconds she would turn around to be sure the red-haired man had not returned and was about to pull her down with the ladder.

She reached the top safely and stared at the last rung. Evidently the stranger had balanced himself on his arches while he was sketching, and left sizable chunks of mud on the wood.

"It's that same mud with the little bits of wood in it!" she said to herself.

Nancy quickly stepped into Ned's bedroom and

closed and locked the window. She now made sure that the other window in his room was fastened, then checked all the windows in the whole house.

She went back to Ned's bedroom, turned the blackboard over, and tested herself on the eye-shaped set of numbers. She was glad she had remembered everything correctly. Nancy now erased the whole design and put the blackboard in the closet.

Just then the telephone rang and Nancy went to answer it. The caller was Bess.

"Where *are* you?" she asked. "We're all getting worried about you."

"Don't worry any longer," Nancy replied. "I'll be over in a few minutes. There's been a little excitement here, but everything is all right now. Bye. See you."

Before leaving, Nancy stood in the living room and reflected on whether or not she had done everything she should.

"The ladder!" she thought. "I mustn't leave that in place. I wonder where the man got it."

The young detective decided to put it in the Nickersons' basement. This accomplished, she called the police and suggested that they keep a watch on the house and nab the owner of the notebook if he returned.

Then Nancy climbed into her car and headed for the restaurant. During the drive her thoughts were on the mud she had seen across the top rung of the ladder.

"I must locate that mucky, swampy place. If Glenn Munson can take me on another flight, perhaps I can find it."

Nancy finally arrived at Flannery's restaurant, where the rest of her group was waiting to have dinner.

She sat down and then said, "I'm dreadfully sorry to be so late."

George spoke up. "Don't keep us in suspense. Tell us what held you up."

As Nancy related what had happened at the house, the others grew more and more astonished.

At the end of her recital, Bess asked, "What did you do with the notebook after you changed the numbers?"

"I left it where I found it and notified the police."

While they were eating, Nancy mentioned her plan of calling Glenn Munson and trying to find the swamp area where Ned might be a prisoner.

Mr. Nickerson had a suggestion. "I'm sure that the Emerson College library must have an excellent collection of books on the geology of this region. Perhaps you can find one that describes mud similar to what you found. In the meantime I'll call the State Forest Commission and see what I can find out."

When they reached home Nancy immediately

went to see if the notebook was still there. It lay where Nancy had put it. A plainclothes policeman at once stepped from behind a tree and said no one had come for it.

"I'll wait a little longer, then take the notebook with me," he told Nancy. "I doubt that its owner will return." Nancy was inclined to agree with him.

Despite her concern, Nancy slept soundly that night. Early the next morning she telephoned Glenn and arranged to take a trip with him the following morning at ten o'clock.

"Sorry I couldn't make it today," he said. "By the way I have some information for you. Evidently the mysterious copter had a phony registration number on it. The authorities haven't been able to identify the owner of the craft. Wish I could have had better news for you. See you tomorrow."

"I'll be there promptly," Nancy promised. "Thanks a lot."

After breakfast the girls said good-by to Mr. and Mrs. Nickerson. There were a few seconds when each thought the others were going to cry, but they all braced themselves and wished the rest good luck in finding Ned.

"You're doing very well, Nancy," said Mr. Nickerson, "and I wish I could have picked up as many clues as you have."

The young detective said she hoped they

would lead somewhere. She and the other girls climbed into her car and took the same route as they had the day before.

Upon reaching Emerson College, Nancy left the cousins at the fraternity house and went on to the campus library alone. She had met the reference librarian several times, so she was admitted on her own identification.

When Nancy told her what book she wanted to consult, Miss Greenleaf directed her to the proper section. For an hour Nancy buried herself in the fascinating subject of geological findings of Emerson and the surrounding area.

Her search for swampy districts was finally rewarded. There were three in different locations outside Emerson.

"Here's one that's in a straight line from my home in River Heights," she decided and read more about it.

Apparently the swamp was an unusual place. There was a hilltop in the center of a large circular area, which was wooded but mucky. The text said that it was impossible to drive through the swamp. The only way to explore it was either on horseback or on foot in high boots.

"But one must watch carefully for dangerous spots that seem to have no bottom," she read. "There are many rotted logs, some of them under the slimy water."

Nancy reread the paragraph. "It sounds like a

good place to avoid," she thought, but immediately decided nothing would keep her away if there was any chance of going in and rescuing Ned.

She returned to the fraternity house just as students were coming in for the lunch hour. Bess, George, Burt, and Dave met her.

"A letter for Burt Eddleton," one of the students sang out.

Burt went to get it from the pile of recently delivered mail on the hall table. He looked at the envelope, then excitedly brought it to show to his friends.

"This is from Ned!" he whispered. "And here on the outside in another handwriting someone has written 'Found on road near Arbutus.' "

"Where is Arbutus?" Bess asked.

No one could answer her question.

Dave said, "Open it."

Quickly Burt slit the envelope and took out the enclosed note. In a hastily scrawled handwriting Ned had written, *Don't know where I am. Prisoner of red-haired nut.*

At once there were conjectures about who the red-haired nut was. Could he be Crosson or perhaps someone else connected with a Cyclops gang?

Bess spoke up. "I still want to know where Arbutus is."

Nancy's trip to the college library suddenly

paid off. "I remember now. It's a small town fairly close to the swamp that I've decided to investigate."

Dave asked how far it was from Emerson.

Nancy replied, "Not far. Let's go to Arbutus in my car right after lunch. We can take it as close as possible to the swamp and then walk the rest of the way."

"The rest of the way to where?" Bess asked.

George spoke up. "The place where Ned may be a prisoner, silly!" she chided her cousin.

Burt stared at the girls' feet. "I hope you brought hiking boots. You'll need them to slosh through a swamp."

Ruefully the girls said they had not packed any, but they would go anyway. Burt winked at Dave but said nothing. An hour later three pairs of men's small-size hiking boots, borrowed from short students in the fraternity house, stood in the guest room.

As Burt drove the group toward Arbutus, they discussed the case again. George wondered how Ned's note had got onto the road. She even suggested that it might have been planted there to lure Ned's friends to a place where they might become prisoners.

"In that case, we'd better not go," said Bess. "Nancy, what do you think?"

The young detective was inclined to believe that in some way Ned had managed to tuck the note in a crack on the outer wall of the mysterious copter.

"He hoped it would fall off while the whirlybird was in flight, and drop where somebody would find it."

"I'll bet you're right," said Dave.

They reached Arbutus, and obtained directions at a gas station to a road which led directly to the swampy area. The attendant looked at them strangely and finally warned the group that the place was dangerous. "People have been known to lose their lives in there."

"We'll watch our step," Nancy assured him.

Burt drove as far as he dared, then parked. They all got out and started off on foot. Even before they reached the woods, the path became almost impassable.

It would not have been possible to proceed in anything but hiking boots. The group was so busy watching the ground that there was no conversation.

Then suddenly Dave cried out, "Look! There goes a copter."

It had risen from behind the hilltop ahead and now flew away. The hikers stopped short. The same thought ran through the minds of everyone. Was Ned aboard the helicopter?

CHAPTER XI

Wilderness Cabin

As the copter turned and flew off, George said, "Come on! Let's follow that pilot!"

Bess looked at her cousin in amazement. "How would you do that?" she asked. "I didn't bring my wings."

The others laughed but Nancy's eyes were focused on the direction the helicopter had taken. It was going in a westerly direction. Where would it land?

Burt spoke up. "Maybe that craft isn't connected with your mystery case, Nancy."

"You could be right," she replied. "But the copter certainly looked like the one that landed on my front lawn. We never could follow it, though. Let's go on to the swamp."

They finally came to the edge of the mucky area and trudged up the hill, which, according to what Nancy had read, stood in the center of the swamp.

The incline was steep. Low-growing bushes and trees, partially withered, grew here and there on the hillside. A lot of shalelike rock made the climb hazardous.

Presently Bess stopped. "This is positively the worst hike I have ever taken."

Her cousin George teased, "It's going to be worse on the other side. Cheer up!"

When the group reached the top of the hill, they surveyed the landscape in front of them. The swamp below looked wider than the one through which they had just come.

When they reached it, the young people also found it was much more treacherous than the other one. They sloshed along in ankle-deep mud, then stopped to wash it off whenever they came to clear pools of water.

It was comparatively still in the wooded swamp, but suddenly a crow took off from the ground with a screech. It landed in a treetop and cawed raucously.

Nancy smiled. "I guess he's warning the flock that there are intruders on his premises."

Though the going was rough, the group did not think about the arduous hike. They became interested in the beauty of nature around them.

"Look over there!" said Dave. "A ringneck pheasant."

The large iridescent bird with the white ring of feathers around its neck did not stir from the log on which it was standing, its long tail sweeping out behind.

"Listen!" George said a few minutes later.

The trekkers stopped and became silent.

"Hear that warbler?" George asked.

They could detect the dainty trilling notes of the warbler's song but it took time for them to find the bird. Finally Bess saw it seated high on the branch of a tree. "There it is!"

Nancy remarked, "From here it looks like a bird without a head. If it weren't for his eyes, you wouldn't know he had one. He looks as if a black mask had been pulled down over the upper part of his head. I guess that's why it is called the hooded warbler."

"Did you know," George asked, "that the female of this species doesn't have a mask? I suppose that's so she'll surely be seen by the boy warblers."

The group laughed and went on. Bess, intrigued by the wildlife, kept looking up. Without warning, she stepped into a deep hole of muddy, greenish water.

Instantly the others pulled her out, but she was a mess. Nancy took several tissues from her pocket and began to clean her friend's legs.

"Ugh!" Bess said suddenly. "Look at these things crawling around on me!"

Dave said kindly, "They won't hurt you. They're only miniature salamanders."

He tore leaves from several bushes and helped wipe off Bess's dungarees and sweater, while George and Nancy worked on the girl's hair.

"What am I going to do?" Bess wailed.

"Grin and bear it," George replied. But she did admit feeling sorry for her cousin.

"I guess from here on I'd better watch my step more carefully," Bess said finally. She was still shaking from her unexpected bath and held Dave's hand tightly for the rest of their trip through the swamp.

Immediately ahead was a small, open field which everyone assumed must be the place from which the helicopter had taken off. Directly beyond was another swampy area. A small cabin painted dark green blended so well with the surrounding growth that it was hardly noticeable.

"That could be the place where Ned is being held!" Nancy said excitedly.

The three girls and their companions walked across the field and gingerly went forward. The ground was spongy, caking their boots with mud, but walking was not as difficult as it had been in the swamp.

No one said anything at first, then George commented, "That swamp sure was an obstacle course, and I don't relish going back through it."

"Nor I," Bess said. "I hope somebody can figure out a different way of getting to the place where we left the car!"

Nobody answered her because all of them were sure they would have to return along the same route.

Nancy hurried in front of the group and walked up to the cabin door. She knocked. No one replied. She pounded loudly but in vain.

"Nobody home," she said. "Unless someone's hiding in there."

Nancy added that it was possible Ned was a prisoner and could not make a sound. He must be rescued!

She tried the door and finding it unlocked, she walked in. Her friends followed. No one was in sight.

All gasped in astonishment. The one-room cabin was a fully equipped electronic laboratory with two cots, a small stove, and well-stocked shelves of canned food.

"Well, Sherlock Holmes," said George to Nancy, "what are your thoughts now?"

Before replying, Nancy began to examine the laboratory. Burt and Dave did also. There were all sorts of gadgets, and open notebooks with numbers which meant nothing to the visitors.

Meanwhile, Bess had been looking around. She announced that there were no clothes in the place. "Do you suppose whoever lives here knew we were coming and skipped out?" she asked.

"Otherwise why would anyone leave all this good food—meat, eggs, milk, and bread? I could eat some of it right now."

Presently Burt and Dave called to the girls to come to a corner of the lab.

"We've discovered a remote-control outfit, and here's the sending set."

"And over there," Dave added, "are a computer and programming tapes."

"Are you saying," George spoke up, "that the robot copter *was* kept here and its movements were controlled from this cabin?"

"It looks that way."

Bess asked, "Do you think Ned, Crosson, and the red-haired nut were in the copter we saw flying away from here?"

"I have a strong feeling," Nancy said, "that Crosson and the red-haired nut are one and the same person. I believe that Ned in his note was trying to tell us that Crosson is crazy and dangerous."

Dave reminded the others that they were just doing a lot of guessing. "We haven't come across one single thing around here to prove who the occupants are."

Nancy agreed with Dave and said that it was important they try to find out. "Let's all hunt for a clue," she proposed.

Everyone went to work. There was complete silence for a long time.

Nancy looked under both cots and pulled them from the wall. Suddenly her eyes fastened upon a mark which had been cut into the wood of the wall. At first glance it seemed to be a W. Was it someone's initial?

She called her friends' attention to it and they came over to look at the initial. Nancy squinted her eyes and stared at it.

Suddenly she said, "This isn't a W. I'm sure it's two N's. And that could stand for Ned Nickerson!"

Bess, George, and the boys leaned over to examine the mark. They all agreed that indeed it was NN.

"This is where Ned must have slept," Burt said. "And I'm convinced he was taken away in the copter we saw leaving here."

"Do any of you think he'll be brought back?" Dave spoke up. "I don't."

No one did, but Burt and Dave were inclined to think that Ned's captor might return. They were of the opinion that he would not leave the valuable equipment unguarded for long, although the possibility of it being taken in this forsaken place was slim.

Nancy was quiet for several minutes while the rest searched some more. When they reported that there were no other clues, she told the group that a possibility of getting to the main road without hiking there had just occurred to her.

"What is it?" Bess asked eagerly. "I certainly would like to be rescued from this creepy place!"

"The quicker the better," George added.

Nancy turned to the boys. "Do you think we could possibly contact the police over the two-way radio set here? We could tell them our suspicions regarding this cabin, and the take-off of the copter." She looked at Bess and grinned. "If they come by helicopter, they might even give us a ride back to our car."

Dave offered to try contacting headquarters.

CHAPTER XII

Hidden Notes

BURT and Dave bent over the sending set, trying to figure out how the various gadgets worked.

"This is a complicated one," Dave remarked.

George, who had had a little coaching along these lines from her father, an electronic engineer, made several valuable suggestions.

"Where are the call letters?" she asked.

The young people examined every inch of the set but could find none.

"I wonder whom the kidnapper was calling? Some pal? Or a member of a Cyclops gang?" George asked.

The boys said they wished they knew and went on with their examination, hoping desperately to get the set to respond. Finally they hit the right combination and in a moment Burt's signal was answered.

He said, "Calling from station without call letters. Who are you?"

The listener seemed reluctant to reply and asked, "Why don't you have call letters? Everybody does."

"We're in trouble here. Owner is away. No clue to call letters," Burt told him.

The ham radio operator turned out to be answering from a town not far away.

Burt told him he was calling from a swamp and then said, "There are five of us here. It's near Arbutus. Will you phone the police department and ask if they'll come out here? We've made an important discovery about a missing person."

Nancy stood listening. She began to shake her head to indicate that Burt had told enough. He nodded and put a finger over his lips to indicate he understood.

"Will you please do this for us?" Burt asked the ham. "I'm Burt Eddleton. I attend Emerson College. You can check there if you like."

The man said he would be glad to help and asked, "Where are you?"

Burt gave him directions from Arbutus, then said, "Over."

Nancy and her friends hoped fervently that the ham would not think the message was some kind of a joke and pay no attention to it.

"There's nothing we can do but wait," said Bess with a sigh.

"In the meantime," Nancy spoke up, "we can continue searching this place."

All but Nancy went outside to look for clues. She felt that if Ned had been outdoors, he would have tried to escape and not bothered, or had time, to leave a clue.

"More than likely he was kept in one spot, either chained up or threatened with dire punishment if he tried to get away. We know he used this cot," Nancy thought, gazing at it for a full minute.

She decided to pull the cot apart to see if anything was hidden inside. First she took off two blankets, shook them vigorously, and looked over every inch of them.

She found nothing. Next, Nancy picked up the mattress and laid it on the floor. To her amazement, she saw dozens of small note-pad sheets with Ned's writing on them lying on the springs. Eagerly she picked up one and read the message which looked as if it had been hurriedly scrawled.

There was a date on the paper. The day Ned was kidnapped!

The note said, "Cannot understand why I was kidnapped when Cyclops could have stolen what he wants if he had waited a little longer."

There were other notes written the following day. One read: "Am being pretty well fed and comfortable, but this madman threatens me with a gun whenever I move."

There was a daily series of notes telling of Ned's treatment, how one ankle was chained to the bed, and his captor's endeavors to keep him away from the lab even when he let him get a little exercise.

Nancy came across an entry with no date on it, but the contents were very enlightening. It said that his kidnapper had prepared the robot helicopter for a flight to Nancy Drew's home.

Ned had begged to see the copter and the man had finally consented and taken him outside. "When my captor was not looking I slipped a note to Nancy onto the floor."

Nancy was elated. "That's mystery number one cleared up!" she murmured.

At this point Bess and George came into the cabin to see if Nancy had learned anything. They were astounded at her discovery of the notes.

"It puzzles me," Bess said, "why the name Crosson doesn't appear in any of these notes."

George replied that it could mean the kidnapper was not Crosson after all. "And he never told Ned his name."

Nancy decided to copy the notes in case the police should come and want them. She had just finished when the girls became aware of a whirring sound in the air. Quickly Nancy stuffed both sets of notes into her pocket. Then she restored the bed to its normal look and went outside.

A police helicopter was arriving. As soon as it

set down, the young people went over to talk to the men. The ham had done what he had promised!

"Tell us everything that has happened," one of the officers said, after three men had alighted.

As quickly as possible, Nancy gave them the highlights of the story and showed them the notes Ned had written, and her copies of them.

"This looks serious," the captain remarked. "I'll take your copies to turn over to the FBI. If we need the originals, I'll let you know. What's the registration number of the copter?"

Nancy replied, "We didn't see it today. But the one we saw the first time turned out to be a fake."

After hearing the story, two of the three officers decided to stay at the cabin in case the suspected kidnapper returned. The pilot told the young people he would take them to their car and to climb aboard.

In a short time Nancy and her friends were delivered to the automobile. They thanked him and he wished them luck. He warned the young people to be careful in their future sleuthing. "The kidnapper sounds like a bad one." The pilot flew off and Burt took the wheel of Nancy's car.

When they reached the fraternity house, Bess could hardly wait to get under the shower. She had said nothing more about her sudden spill in the swamp, but she felt very itchy.

The other girls washed and changed too, then joined the boys for dinner. When they finished eating, Burt and Dave said that they had to attend a night lecture.

"Sorry not to be here to entertain you girls," Dave said. "But we'll make up for it some time. Promise."

Bess laughed. "I've had enough entertainment for one day! See you when you get back from your lecture."

She and George went off to talk to some of the other boys. Nancy was torn between her desire to stay with them and a sudden feeling of curiosity about Ned's notes. There might be some clues in them which she had not noticed!

In the guest room she sat down and reread the notes, then examined each one through her magnifying glass. But she could detect no hints to Ned's whereabouts, nor to why he had been kidnapped.

Nancy sat staring into space. Then on a sudden hunch she closed the door to the hall and turned off all the lights. She almost yelled aloud in surprise. Drawn in the corner of one note in fluorescent ink was an exact duplicate of the mysterious glowing eye she had seen at the Anderson Museum!

"How strange!" Nancy thought.

She began to wonder whether Ned had put this on the paper sometime before his kidnapping, or if by some ruse he had been able to use certain materials in the cabin's lab.

Then Nancy remembered that one note indicated Ned was not allowed far from his cot. The paper with the glowing eye must have been from a note pad her friend was carrying when he arrived at the isolated cabin.

"The message on the paper doesn't light up, so it probably has nothing to do with the glowing eye," she thought.

Nancy had just turned all the lights back on when the door opened and George and Bess came in.

Instantly Nancy said, "I'll show you something very interesting. Turn off all the lights!"

When Bess and George saw the glowing eye on the paper, they stared in disbelief. Nancy told them she wondered if Ned had put the glowing eye on the sheet as some sort of clue for her.

"What I wish I could do right now is figure out where he is at this moment. Oh dear! We came so close to rescuing him."

Bess put an arm around Nancy. "Don't be sad. We'll track him down yet."

George suggested that the kidnapper probably would bring Ned back to the cabin as soon as he thought it was safe.

"He'll never guess that two officers are there waiting to capture him and set Ned free," she said.

Bess, who had been staring at the glowing eye, asked Nancy if she thought the drawing on the notepaper might indicate something special about his work.

"Yes. I think Ned has invented something unique and tried it out on this paper," Nancy replied as she turned on the light. "It may or may not have anything to do with the glowing eye in the museum. When he found it worked, he began to make a bigger and better one. At that point someone decided to get hold of the invention and put it to his own use, maybe even sell the formula."

Just then Burt and Dave entered the room. At once George suggested that they close the door and turn off the light.

The boys laughed. Dave said, "What's going on?"

"Wait until you see something amazing Nancy found," George replied.

The boys were as astounded at the discovery as the girls had been.

"It may not be long before we hear something important," Bess told the boys. "Ned's kidnapper may go back to that cabin and be captured by the police."

Nancy, however, said she had a different idea.

"What is it, Nancy?" George asked excitedly.

CHAPTER XIII

The Escape

"Here is my idea," Nancy said to her waiting friends. "We're sure Crosson uses the old farmhouse. If he's the kidnapper, he might have taken Ned there."

"It's a good guess," George conceded.

Bess suggested that maybe Crosson would put Ned in the clothes chute. No one would be likely to look for a missing person in that spot.

"Another good guess," Dave remarked, smiling at Bess.

George spoke up. "Then we should rescue Ned at once!"

"Yes," Nancy agreed. "And I have another hunch. Crosson may stay there only until early morning. Which of you is game to go with me right now?"

Everyone in the group was eager to leave immediately. Burt did the driving, which gave Nancy a chance to mull over the many angles to the mystery. The red-haired man had outwitted her and she was determined he would not do it again. She sighed, however. He was very clever and surely would try to outsmart them.

"Oh, oh!" Burt burst out. "Look ahead! Block-ade!"

By now they were about half a mile from the farmhouse. A wall of piled-up stones stretched across the road. Atop the center of it was a red lantern. Attached below was a large sign which read:

DANGER
BLASTING AHEAD

There was no way to get around the wall at this point because trees grew rather solidly along the road.

Bess asked, "What are we going to do?"

Burt said he would drive around via another road and approach the farmhouse from the opposite direction. It took twenty minutes to do this. When they came within half a mile of the far side of the building, they were confronted with a great pile of brush across the road. The sides had high embankments.

"Stymied again!" George remarked.

Nancy pointed out the fact that there were no

"What are we going to do?" Bess asked.

trees along the road in this area. "Let's walk and approach the house through the field," she proposed.

Bess reminded her that it probably would be rough walking. "What's the matter with the road? That's smooth!"

Nancy said it was possible there was some truth in the sign at the stone barrier. The road might be torn up or have unexploded dynamite stored on it. However, she was suspicious that the person who put up the sign and the two barriers had done so to keep visitors away.

"Why not notify the police and let them take care of everything?" Bess suggested.

"But Ned may be a prisoner at the farmhouse," George reminded her. "Well, I'm ready to start. Who's willing to go along? I promise an adventure!"

"I'll wait in the car," Bess said.

Dave decided to stay with her. "It's too dangerous for Bess to be alone here."

The others left them, climbed the embankment on the farmhouse side, and walked through the field. It was bright moonlight, so flashlights were not needed. The rutted ground could be spotted easily, so Burt and the girls had no trouble reaching the farmhouse quickly. They had walked as lightly as possible and not said a word.

The abandoned house was in darkness. As the

group skirted a small brook and copse of trees they found themselves approaching the building from the rear.

Suddenly Nancy stopped short and pointed. The others looked ahead. Clearly outlined in the bright moonlight was a helicopter!

Burt whispered to Nancy, "Is it the robot copter?"

"Yes. If Crosson and Ned came in the copter, they must be here!"

The three young people started to run forward, but before they got very far, the rotors of the copter began to whir, and with a roar the craft lifted from the ground.

Nancy could not refrain from shouting, "Ned, are you there? Ned, are you aboard?"

Her friends took up the cry, but there was no answer or signal. Because of the noise, had the person or persons aboard been unable to hear them, or did they not want to answer? Perhaps there was no one in the craft! If so, was the person who had programmed it, on the premises?

Nancy and the others walked to the house. The front door was unlocked, so they entered. Beaming their flashlights, they searched every room thoroughly, watchful not to be captured themselves should an enemy be lurking in the house.

Finally, after hunting everywhere, even in the clothes chute, Nancy said, "Ned isn't a prisoner here, so I believe he was in that copter. How I wish I knew where he was being taken!"

One thing she was sure of—the helicopter had not been headed for the swamp area, so unless the pilot made a change in direction, he was not going to the cabin. But where was he going?

"We'd better notify the police," Burt suggested. "Two of the kidnapper's hiding places will be covered."

"Which means," George added, "that sooner or later he and Ned are bound to be found."

"Unless," Nancy suggested, "Ned's red-haired captor has still other hiding places."

"We may as well go back to the car," Burt said. He told Bess and Dave what had happened, then suggested they all return to the fraternity house.

On the way he stopped in town at police headquarters and Nancy hurried inside to tell her story. The captain on duty promised to send out men not only to wait for the return of Ned and his abductor, but also to scan every inch of the road that had been closed off.

"If we find it okay, we'll take down the barriers so the road can be opened again to traffic," the officer said.

"From what you tell me," he went on, "I imagine someone stood over your friend Ned with some kind of a firearm and made him do all the work of building those barriers."

Nancy smiled. "I agree. What I'm hoping is

that Ned will not be badly mistreated before we find him."

She gave the captain her home telephone number and also that of Ned's fraternity house at Emerson College.

"If I have any news," the captain said, "I'll call you at once."

When she and her friends reached the campus, Nancy suddenly was reminded of her date with Glenn Munson the following morning for a flight in his helicopter.

"There's not much use in going now," she thought. "We found the wilderness hiding place."

The young detective wondered how she could put the flying time to good use by doing some sleuthing. Suddenly an idea came to her.

"Why don't I take the copter to River Heights and talk to Dad and Marty King?" she asked herself. "Both of them might have some information for me they wouldn't want to talk about on the phone."

Nancy told the other girls what she had in mind, and early the next morning Burt drove her out to the airfield to meet Glenn. He was already there.

"I've changed my plans," Nancy told him. "Would you mind flying to River Heights and spending a little time there?"

The young pilot grinned. "Nothing would suit me better," he replied.

Burt drove off and Nancy climbed into the helicopter. In a few minutes she and Glenn were in the air headed for River Heights.

"Why this sudden change of plans?" he asked her.

Nancy told him about what she and her friends had found at the wilderness hiding place.

"Unfortunately the people there took off in a copter just before we reached the place," she added.

In a short while Glenn landed his craft at River Heights Airport. Nancy said that she wanted to go home first to see if there were any mail or messages for her.

"At your command." The young man grinned as they walked toward a taxi.

Nancy gave her address and soon they were winding through the residential area of the small city.

"One more block and we're there," she announced as the taxi turned onto a street lined with attractive homes and sycamore trees.

By the time Nancy alighted from the taxi Hannah Gruen was rushing out the front door. She stopped short in amazement when she saw Nancy and Glenn.

"I thought for a moment you had come back with Ned!" she exclaimed, glancing in embarrassment at Nancy's companion.

Nancy introduced Glenn, and the three went

into the house. The young detective gave Hannah the highlights of her recent adventures.

The housekeeper frowned as she listened. Finally she remarked, "That kidnapper is a slippery eel!"

She changed the subject abruptly and said she would prepare luncheon for Nancy and Glenn. "How long can you stay?"

Nancy said she was uncertain. "I want to go downtown and talk to Dad and Marty King. If we're coming back here to eat, I'll phone you. In the meantime, will you keep your eyes and ears open for anything—"

Hannah interrupted with a laugh. "Will do!" she said. "News or clues for Nancy Drew!"

"Now I want you to meet my dad," Nancy told Glenn.

The couple walked downtown to Mr. Drew's offices. As they entered, Miss Hanson, his long-time secretary, greeted them pleasantly.

After Nancy had introduced Glenn, she asked, "Is Dad in?"

Miss Hanson shook her head. "He went out a few minutes ago."

"Then I'll talk to Marty King," Nancy said.

"Sorry," Miss Hanson replied, "but she went with your father. I believe they were going to the bank first, and then to lunch."

Nancy tried hard not to show how upset she was by this information. Not willing to give up on trying to talk to her father, she inquired where they were going to eat.

"I don't know," Miss Hanson said. "Do you want to leave a message?"

Nancy asked the secretary if she had heard Marty King say anything about the mystery which she was trying to solve.

Again, Miss Hanson shook her head. With a faint smile, she remarked, "Marty rarely tells me anything."

Nancy said she would come back in a couple of hours. In the meantime, she and Glenn would return to the house for lunch. She picked up Miss Hanson's telephone and called Hannah.

"We'll be back to have lunch," she said. "Anything you want me to pick up in town? Dessert, perhaps?"

"I think not. Your dad ordered a special one for dinner. I'll serve some of it to you."

"What is it?" Nancy asked.

Hannah laughed. "It's one of your favorites too. I want to surprise you."

Nancy and Glenn walked back. As soon as they had finished eating Hannah's delicious lemon meringue pie, Nancy went to phone the Faynes and Marvins and tell them the latest news about their daughters. When she called the Fayne home, George's father answered.

"Hello?"

"Hello. This is Nancy. I flew home for a few hours and I thought you and Mrs. Fayne would like to know how we're progressing on the case."

"Indeed we would."

When Nancy finished telling him, Mr. Fayne said, "Nancy, I, too, have some information in which I'm sure you will be vitally interested!"

CHAPTER XIV

Chilly Conference

MR. FAYNE told Nancy that the previous day he had been on a business trip to Martin City.

"I had finished my conference early, so I decided to run out to the Anderson Museum at Hager and take a look at that glowing eye you girls talked about."

"What did you think of it?" Nancy asked him.

His answer surprised her. "It wasn't there."

"You mean somebody took it?" Nancy exclaimed. "But who?"

George's father told her that when he went into the museum he had introduced himself to Miss Wilkin. "I said that I'd like to see the glowing eye which my daughter had viewed there a few days before.

"The woman at once became very nervous," he reported. "She said there was no such thing at the museum. When I insisted, she finally admitted that the eye had been removed."

"By whom?" Nancy asked quickly.

Mr. Fayne replied that Miss Wilkin had said she had no idea. It had happened when she was off the premises, and she had assumed that it had been taken back by the Emerson College authorities.

Nancy was amazed to hear this. "What else did Miss Wilkin tell you?" she asked Mr. Fayne.

"Something that contradicts what you were told—that no student from Emerson had been there in a long time."

"Anything else?" Nancy asked Mr. Fayne.

"No, nothing else, so I left the museum. But I thought you'd want to know what I had learned."

"I certainly do," Nancy replied, puzzled over this latest turn of events.

She thanked Mr. Fayne for giving her the information. As soon as she finished the phone call, she dialed Professor Titus. He was as surprised as the young detective had been upon hearing Miss Wilkin's story.

"One thing she's right about. No student from my department has gone there to study in a long time. The glowing eye never reached the college. There is no reason why it should, since it isn't our property."

He and Nancy discussed this new angle of the

mystery, then the professor said, "Could you meet me at the museum at four o'clock? I'd like to find out more about this whole thing."

"Please hold the line a couple of minutes while I talk with the pilot who flew me over here. I'll see if he can take me to Hager."

She put down the phone and went to talk to Glenn, who was looking at a wall picture of an early biplane. In answer to Nancy's question, he said he would be glad to take her on the errand. Nancy relayed this to Professor Titus and then said, "I'll see you at four."

Nancy and Glenn walked back to Mr. Drew's office. The lawyer still had not returned.

"But Marty King is here," Miss Hanson told her. "Want to talk to her?"

"Yes."

Turning to Glenn, Nancy said, "Will you excuse me a few minutes while I see Marty?"

The pilot nodded. "Watch the time, though," he advised. "Remember your four-o'clock date."

"I will," Nancy promised, and opened Marty King's door. "Hello," she said. "I'm sorry I missed you before and that Dad is not here now. Tell me, how is he?"

"He seems fine," Marty replied. "Is there some message I can give him?"

"No, but I thought I'd bring both of you up to date on the glowing eye mystery."

Marty King leaned forward in her desk chair.

Nancy asked, "Marty, when did you last hear from your contact?"

The young lawyer did not answer at once. She seemed to be searching for an answer. Finally she said, "Why—uh—not recently."

Nancy decided to catch this secretive young woman off guard if possible. Looking directly at her, she asked, "When did you last hear from Zapp Crosson?"

Marty was so amazed that she gave a convulsive start and did not reply. She jumped from her chair and came from behind the desk. Her eyes were flashing.

"I don't know how you learned about him," she said, "but I'll tell you this. I found out he's a red-haired nut!"

Excitedly Nancy thought, "Those were Ned's exact words in his note to Burt!"

"So I've heard," Nancy said aloud. "What I want to know, Marty, is when did you last see him? Recently?"

"I haven't seen him in a while and don't want to—ever again," Marty said angrily.

Nancy felt that she had the advantage and pressed on with her queries. "When did you last hear from Zapp Crosson?"

At this, Marty tossed her head into the air and a smug expression came over her face. "Next thing I know you'll be asking me what he told me about the glowing eye."

"I did have that in mind," Nancy admitted with a little smile. "Well, how about my other question? When did you last hear from your contact Zapp Crosson?"

"I won't tell you," the young lawyer said defiantly.

"As you like," Nancy replied. "But I want to tell you that Crosson might be involved in a kidnapping case."

"Oh, you mean your boy friend?" Marty King shot back. "Well, I'm sure Zapp had nothing whatever to do with it."

Marty King looked a little frightened at the information. "I'll tell you this. Zapp pesters me with letters but I don't answer them."

Nancy asked her where the letters had been mailed.

Marty replied, "Most of them were postmarked Emerson."

Nancy stared into space. This meant that Crosson was still in the general area from where Ned had been taken. She must concentrate all her efforts in that vicinity to find him!

For a few seconds Nancy was tempted to confide in Marty. But a feeling of distrust about the girl swept over her and she changed her mind.

"I must go now," Nancy said. "Thank you, Marty, for your helpful information. And I think I should warn you again: Zapp Crosson is in bad trouble—very bad trouble."

"What do you mean?" Marty asked. "Are you implying that he is a suspect in the kidnapping?"

"Yes," Nancy said.

For the next few minutes there was a verbal exchange between the two girls which revealed nothing of importance to either one. Marty prodded Nancy to tell her more about Crosson but the young sleuth was evasive. Finally she said she must leave because of her next appointment.

Marty King walked with her to the door and Nancy politely introduced Glenn Munson. The young lawyer's eyebrows lifted and Nancy could imagine her saying, "Where did you meet this handsome young man?"

Nancy was amused but merely said, "Tell Dad I'm sorry I missed him. Good-by. And good-by to you, Miss Hanson."

Nancy and Glenn hurried off and in a little while they were airborne and heading for Hager. The pilot set his whirlybird down in an airfield not far from the Anderson Museum and locked the ignition.

As they jumped out, he said, "I hope I'm not intruding, but I have a feeling you could use a little extra protection. Mind if I go along?"

"I wish you would," she said.

Professor Titus was waiting in front of the building. "You're right on schedule," he said. "Well, let's go inside and see what we can learn."

Nancy introduced Glenn and the three entered the building. Miss Wilkin gave the visitors her usual icy reception and informed them that the museum would be closing for the night at four-thirty.

Nancy spoke up. "Your booklet says you stay open until five o'clock."

Miss Wilkin replied, "At times we make exceptions. Tonight is one of them."

Nancy tried not to show that the woman's chilly attitude annoyed her. She said, "We'd like to explore a little while."

"All right, but watch the signs and don't touch anything you're not supposed to," the prim woman ordered them.

Nancy at once led Professor Titus and Glenn to the narrow hallway behind the wall where she had seen the glowing eye. Glenn searched the wall for a switch that might activate any machinery. He found one and turned the switch but nothing happened. With sensitive fingers he moved along, trying again and again to locate another possible contact, but without success.

Professor Titus had gone around to the big room where the glowing eye had shone high on the wall. Nancy, meanwhile, had found a sliding panel in the wall near where Glenn was looking and saw a closet. There was nothing in it.

The young detective stepped inside. "Maybe there's some kind of a switch in here," she said to herself and began running one hand over the wall.

Suddenly her fingers felt strange and she tried to pull them away. But she was not able to do so. Her whole hand was drawn against the wall. She tugged harder but still could not move it. Before she could call out to Glenn, the panel closed.

Instinct told Nancy she was in serious trouble. At the top of her lungs she cried, "Help! Help!"

CHAPTER XV

Abrupt Resignation

WHILE Nancy, terror-stricken, continued to yell for help, Glenn and Professor Titus tried to find her. She was hidden from sight and they did not know where to look. The closet she was in stifled her voice.

The trapped girl felt herself becoming faint. A fleeting thought crossed her mind: if she slumped she might be able to pull her hand away from the wall. Without losing her balance, she leaned backward creating a great deal of pressure on her hand. It did not budge.

"Help!" she cried, but this time rather feebly.

By now Glenn had traced her voice and slid open the closet door.

"What's the matter?" he asked.

"I—I can't—get—my—hand—loose!" Nancy whispered.

At that moment Professor Titus arrived. While Nancy was trying to tell him what had happened, Glenn dashed off to find Miss Wilkin. She was seated at the reception desk in the hall.

"Quick!" Glenn exclaimed. "Turn off all the power! Miss Drew is pinned to the wall!"

The prim custodian looked at him blankly and did not move. "Is this some kind of a joke?" she asked.

"No, no!" Glenn assured her. "Nancy is in real trouble. Please turn off all the power in this building!"

Miss Wilkin jumped into action. She grabbed the keys from the desk drawer and rushed down the main hall and around the corner. Glenn raced after her.

The woman reached a large panelboard on the wall and unlocked the covering to it. Quickly she pulled down several levers. At once the place was in darkness.

Glenn did not wait for her to return to the lobby. There was still enough daylight sifting through the windows so that he could easily make his way back to Nancy. The young pilot sighed in relief as he found her seated on the floor, released from the magnetized wall. Professor Titus was kneeling beside her and massaging her hands vigorously.

"Are you all right?" Glenn asked solicitously.

Nancy gave a wan smile. "I will be as soon as the circulation is restored to my hand and arm. They're numb."

Professor Titus kept massaging them for another three minutes, then asked Glenn to take over. The young man seated himself on the floor and began to rub Nancy's hand and arm vigorously.

"That feels great!" she said. "Thank you both so much. I don't know what would have happened to me if you hadn't come to my rescue."

Glenn grinned. "You'd have thought of something," he replied. "Just the same I'm glad you gave me a chance to help you."

By this time Miss Wilkin had come back to the visitors. Nancy explained what had happened to her and asked for an explanation.

The woman turned pale. "I have no idea. This place is getting very spooky and I don't like it."

Miss Wilkin seemed to soften a little. She leaned over Nancy and asked how she was feeling.

"I'm practically well again," the young detective replied.

As Glenn continued to massage her hand and arm, he asked, "Please tell us exactly how it felt when your hand was pinned to the wall."

Nancy said she had suffered small electric shocks before. "But this was different. It didn't go racing through me as the others did. The effect was more like that of a magnet drawing my hand tighter and tighter against the wall. I guess instinct told me not to lean on it. Otherwise my whole side might have been glued to that panel."

Professor Titus wrinkled his brow as if in deep thought. Then he said, "Is the wall covered?"

Glenn went to look. "Yes, with wallpaper."

The science professor said he believed that under the paper there was a metal plate on a screen attached to the wall itself. "Nancy must have been standing on some electric conducting material."

Again Glenn went to peer into the closet. He reported, "There is a rug on the floor."

Professor Titus nodded. "Most likely it's made of an electric conducting material. The hidden plate in the wall is no doubt positive and Nancy is negative. These unlike charges create a strong electrical force which pulled Nancy's hand to the wall and held it there.

"Somewhere in the building there must be a control device which regulates the flow of electric current. In this case, there was enough to pin Nancy's hand to the wall but not enough to hurt her permanently."

Miss Wilkin had listened carefully. Now she seemed paler than ever. "I do not feel very well," she said. "I would appreciate all of you leaving at once. I will close the museum and go home."

Glenn assisted Nancy to her feet and held her arm tightly as the trio walked toward the front door.

Assured that Nancy was all right, Miss Wilkin dashed ahead of them and in a couple of minutes the lights were on once more in the museum. As Nancy neared the entrance, she noticed a pile of booklets on a table nearby. There was a sign alongside them, inviting visitors to help themselves.

The young detective picked one up and found that it contained a history of the museum and a list of its present officers.

Before leaving, Glenn said to Miss Wilkin, "I'd like to investigate that strange wall tomorrow. I'm an expert mechanic and know a lot about electricity and other sources of power."

The custodian cut him short. "I'm sorry but I couldn't allow that. I want no more casualties. In fact, I feel that you people should not come here again."

Nancy and Professor Titus looked at each other but made no comment. They said good-by and left the building. The professor had his car and offered to take Nancy to the fraternity house.

She accepted but said, "I noticed in this booklet that the president of the museum lives in Martin City and has an insurance office there. Glenn, could you take me over there tomorrow morning to call on him? His name is Mr. Schneider and here is the address on Main Street."

"I'll be glad to, of course," Glenn replied. "What time would you like to take off?"

"Is nine o'clock okay?"

"Perfect."

He said good-by to Nancy and Professor Titus and with a grin added, "Nancy, I believe now what your friends say about you—that you never go anywhere without having an adventure."

She laughed and waved as he took a shortcut toward the airfield to get to his helicopter. She and Professor Titus went to his car and they drove to the Omega Chi Epsilon house.

When Nancy walked into the guest room, Bess and George were there changing clothes. They looked at her hard, then Bess exclaimed, "Nancy, something has happened to you! You're as white as a sheet!"

Nancy flopped onto the bed and stretched out. "I do feel a little worn out," she admitted.

Briefly and haltingly, she told what had occurred at the museum.

Bess gasped. "Nancy, you might have been killed!" she exclaimed.

George felt Nancy's pulse. "I don't think you need a doctor," she said. "But your pulse is on the slow side. I recommend you stay in bed until tomorrow morning."

Nancy did not argue. All she wanted to do was go to sleep. She realized the shock to her nervous system had been greater than she at first thought. Knowing how much good Glenn's massaging of her arm had done, she asked George to give her a stimulating rubdown.

George complied at once. She had learned some

physiotherapy techniques through a course in gymnastics. Within minutes Nancy was asleep.

It was nearly ten o'clock that evening when she awakened. Nancy opened her eyes to see Bess, George, Burt, and Dave in the room. They had not made a sound and were watching Nancy carefully to make sure she was all right.

With vigor that startled her friends Nancy sat up and rubbed her eyes. "Hi, everybody!" she said. "You all can stop worrying. I'm fine." She grinned. "I'm hungry. It must be very late, but is there any chance of getting something to eat?"

Her friends were so relieved to hear this good report that each one offered to prepare something for her. Burt and Dave waved Bess and George aside. "We know what Nancy likes," Burt said. "We'll get her something to eat and maybe we'll bring a snack for the rest of us."

The boys brought an excellent meal of hamburgers on buns and a fancy fruit-and-ice cream parfait. It was a relaxing end to a trying day. Relieved and happy that Nancy was all right, the group finally said good night.

The following morning Bess and George drove Nancy out to the airfield to meet Glenn. They took off at once and were in Martin City before ten o'clock. Glenn inquired the way to Main Street and found Mr. Schneider's office. Fortunately he was not in conference and said he would see the callers at once.

Henry Schneider was a good-looking, pleasant man. "Please sit down," he said. "What can I do for you?"

Nancy began her story by saying she was interested in the Anderson Museum, and its mystery. In trying to solve it, she herself had had a frightening experience.

"A mystery you say?" the insurance officer asked.

"Don't you know anything about it?" Nancy queried in surprise.

The man shook his head. "I must admit I seldom go to the museum. I depend on Miss Wilkin to keep me posted."

"And you haven't heard about what happened yesterday afternoon?" Glenn spoke up.

"No, I haven't," Mr. Schneider replied. "Please tell me everything."

Nancy gave him the details of her first visit to the museum when the glowing eye had appeared on a wall. Then she told about going there the previous day, after learning from Mr. Fayne that the glowing eye had been removed.

Nancy went on. "Miss Wilkin assumed that students from Emerson who had been working there had taken it. When she showed the list of names to Professor Titus, he said that not one of them attended Emerson."

"This is amazing," Mr. Schneider remarked. "A small group of young men headed by a somewhat older man with red hair came here a few months ago and asked if they might rent a small corner of the museum to carry on some harmless experiments."

Glenn smiled. "They're far from harmless." He told the insurance man what had happened to Nancy.

Mr. Schneider's eyes opened wide. "This is criminal!" he said. "I'll certainly try to track down these people."

He turned to Nancy. "In the meantime, I'll warn Miss Wilkin not to let anybody into the museum without proper credentials. By the way, Nancy, you haven't told me how you first became interested in it?"

The young detective explained that her father was a lawyer and had a case which indirectly involved the museum. "I don't know what it is specifically, but Dad asked me to try to find out something about the mystery, so I came up here."

At that moment Mr. Schneider's phone rang. He excused himself and answered the call. He listened a moment and then declared, "You can't do that!"

He listened a few minutes, frowning deeply. Finally he said, "Well, if you insist, but I'll have to figure it out. I'll send you a check for the amount I owe you."

He said good-by and put the phone down.

"That was Miss Wilkin," he explained. "She has resigned!"

"What!" Glenn exclaimed.

Nancy told the insurance man that Miss Wilkin had complained last evening of not feeling well. "Maybe she's ill," the young detective said.

"Possibly," Mr. Schneider replied, "but I believe this mystery you've been talking about is partly responsible for her sudden resignation. Why, that museum has been her pet for years! Something must have frightened the woman dreadfully to make her leave in such a hurry."

Nancy remarked that perhaps Miss Wilkin knew more about the strange events there than she cared to tell. "I think I'll go see her. Where does she live?"

Mr. Schneider replied, "Miss Wilkin said she was calling from somewhere else—that she had left town and did not know when she would return."

Nancy sat lost in thought. Here was a new angle to the mystery! Was Miss Wilkin involved in the strange affair?

The young detective was brought out of her reverie by a remark from Mr. Schneider. "Miss Wilkin didn't go to the museum this morning so the place is closed. That's unfortunate. I guess it will have to remain shut until we can get someone else to act as hostess."

A sudden idea flashed into Nancy's mind. "Mr. Schneider," she said, "I have two girl friends staying at Emerson with me while we work on the mystery. Would you consider letting us pinch-hit for Miss Wilkin?"

Mr. Schneider thought about the offer for several seconds, then said, "That's very good of you, but frankly I wish we could invite a scientist to try finding an explanation to what has been going on."

Nancy told him that perhaps Professor Titus could come.

"Excellent idea," Mr. Schneider said. "Can you call him from here?"

Nancy nodded. In a few minutes she had Professor Titus on the line. He readily accepted the invitation to work at the museum for a while. Mr. Schneider was delighted to hear this.

"The sooner I get back the better," Nancy said. "Thank you for seeing us. My friends and I will try to do a good job for you."

He smiled. "And solve that mystery," he replied.

He took a key from a filing cabinet and an architect's drawings of the museum. "These should help you," he said, "but do be careful. I don't want you to injure yourself again."

Nancy promised. Then she and Glenn said good-by and left the insurance office. They went back to the airfield and Glenn took Nancy to

Emerson. As they parted, he held her hand and added, "Any time you need me, let me know and I'll come flying in."

She smiled her appreciation and said, "I'll do just that."

She phoned Bess and George and they came to pick her up. When they heard about their new assignment, the cousins were excited, but Bess was leery of the job.

"Goodness only knows what may happen to us!"

"Don't be chicken," George said to her. "All this is not only going to solve the mystery but also capture the real villain."

"That's right," Nancy said quietly, "and in turn lead us to Ned."

CHAPTER XVI

Astonishing Discovery

THAT evening the young people discussed every angle of the tangled mystery but always came back to the subject of Ned Nickerson. Where was he?

Burt said, "I'm sure Crosson, or whoever kidnapped Ned, knows that two hiding places are under surveillance. He'd be stupid to return to either one."

George spoke up. "Then where would he go?"

"I wish I knew!" Burt replied. "But I feel strongly that Crosson may ditch the copter somewhere and hide out in a new place with Ned."

Dave remarked with a groan that this would mean practically starting all over again to solve the mystery.

"Yes," Bess agreed. "Oh dear! We haven't any clues left to follow. What are we going to do?"

Up to now Nancy had said nothing. An idea was formulating in her mind, however.

Finally George said, "Nancy Drew, what's whirling around in that brain of yours? You have the kind of faraway look you get when you're planning to go off on a new tack."

Nancy smiled. "I admit I'm thinking about a another approach to the mystery. Give me time. If nothing comes of my plan, I don't want to be shown up before you other detectives!"

Her friends laughed and Bess asked, "On how many occasions have you been wrong? I can't think of any."

Dave said, "Nancy's hunches usually turn out to be right, but at times"—he paused—"she has some harrowing experiences before drawing her mystery to a conclusion!"

Pretty soon everyone began to yawn and finally good nights were exchanged. Burt told the girls that he and Dave had an appointment after Sunday chapel services the next day. "We may not see you in the morning. You're going to the museum, aren't you?"

Nancy nodded and said if anything unusual or exciting happened she would telephone the boys.

Directly after breakfast the following morning the girls tidied their room, then drove off to pick up Professor Titus. After greeting them all he climbed into the front seat with Nancy, who headed for the chapel. When the service was over they drove directly to the Anderson Museum.

Professor Titus turned to Nancy. "Are you going to solve the mystery today?" he asked with a twinkle in his eyes.

"Why not?" she bantered. Then, becoming serious, she added, "The authorities haven't captured Zapp Crosson with Ned and we all think that the kidnapper has a new hideout."

"And we haven't the vaguest idea where it is," Bess spoke up, "although I personally suspect Nancy has a hunch."

Nancy made no comment and in a little while they reached the museum. She unlocked the front entrance and they all went in. Professor Titus snapped on the hall light.

"Nancy," he said, "suppose you give us each a job to do. I am not very well acquainted with the exhibits here. Perhaps I should familiarize myself with them in order to be able to answer any questions visitors might ask."

Nancy said that she had formulated a plan of action for the group, but it had more to do with solving the mystery than it did with visitors.

"I suggest that Bess sit here at the hall desk where Miss Wilkin used to be. Bess, you take the admission money and hand each caller one of these visitors' maps of the building."

George suggested that her cousin study each newcomer carefully. If she felt suspicious about any person, she immediately was to call her friends to the lobby.

Nancy asked Professor Titus if he would go into the room where they had seen the glowing eye and watch the wall carefully.

"If anything unusual takes place, give a shrill whistle and we'll all come running."

George spoke up. "What's my assignment?"

Nancy said that she and George would explore upstairs. "I guess it's not part of the museum itself because Miss Wilkin didn't mention it as such and the map with directions to the exhibits shows only the first floor."

"How do we get to the second floor?" George asked. "I don't see a stairway anywhere."

The young detective told her that they would have to hunt for it. She pointed out that the little map had an ST on a spot in the rear hall which probably indicated a door leading to a stairway.

The two girls went off and soon found the door. It opened easily and revealed a rather steep set of steps. Nancy led the way to the second floor, where there were several bedrooms with baths.

Nancy and George went from one to another. They were in perfect order and did not seem to have been used recently.

"I guess nobody slept up here," George said as they came to the last room. "Oh, oh, I was wrong," she added suddenly.

Though there were no clothes in sight, the bed looked as if it had been hastily and badly made and there were soiled towels carelessly slung over racks in the bathroom.

Nancy remarked that she was sure Miss Wilkin had not stayed in the room. "She's too neat to have left the place looking like this."

"Then who was it?" George asked. "I'll bet you're thinking of Zapp Crosson."

Nancy smiled. "Yes, I'm thinking just that. But I'm also wondering if Ned was with him."

George said she doubted it because Ned would have left some kind of clue hoping Nancy would find it. Both girls began a thorough search of bureau drawers and even pulled the bed apart. They found nothing to help solve the mystery.

"I don't think," George said, "Miss Wilkin knew anyone was using the place for diabolic schemes. Zapp probably worked on his weird inventions when she was not on duty."

"On the other hand," Nancy countered, "Miss Wilkin may have been intimidated by him to keep still, but our sleuthing frightened her and she resigned in a hurry."

Perplexed, the girls started to walk back to the stairway. At that moment they heard a thud on the third floor. The two young detectives stared at each other. Was the intruder up there?

Both girls had noticed a door which probably

led to the third floor. Nancy tried to open it but the door was locked.

"I'd like to look up there," Nancy said. "Maybe there's a key to this door downstairs somewhere."

Before going there to hunt for it, George said she would look in all the furniture drawers on the second floor. Nancy assisted but the girls had no luck. In the meantime, there were no further sounds from the third floor.

"Perhaps no one's up there," George decided. "Something just gave way and fell."

The girls went to the first floor and began another search. When they came to the entrance hall, they asked Bess to look in the desk. There was no key in it.

"Did you hear a thud upstairs?" George asked her cousin.

Bess nodded. "I thought one of you knocked something over."

"It was on the third floor," George told her. "We were on the second."

Bess made a face and hunched her shoulders. "More spookiness. I'll be glad when five o'clock comes. We haven't had a single visitor. Maybe other people have had strange experiences here."

Nancy and George went into the large room where Professor Titus was on guard. He reported nothing had happened, but said he too had heard the thud and had assumed the girls had caused it.

When he learned otherwise, he did not take it lightly.

"Somebody may be up there. If so, we should call the police."

Nancy said she would like to investigate the third floor before doing this. "Perhaps there's a ladder in the basement, and I can climb up."

She and the other girls found none. Nancy suggested that they hunt for a secret stairway to the third floor. "Let's examine the chimney in the center of the house first."

They made a search but stayed away from the wall which had proved dangerous for Nancy. Once more they met with disappointment.

"Now will you please give in, Nancy?" the professor urged. "One of us should call the police."

"All right," she said, and went to the entrance lobby to put in the call.

At once Bess spoke up, "Don't use the phone. It's dead. I tried to call the boys at the fraternity house. But come over here. I have something very exciting to show you!"

Nancy, George, and Professor Titus hurried to the desk where Bess was seated.

"I made a discovery," she said. "After you asked me to look for the key, I thought I'd make a better search in the drawer and I found this!"

She showed the others a handwritten book of verses and began to read some of them.

"They're weird!" Professor Titus remarked. "Who wrote these?"

In answer Bess opened the book to the first page. Written on it was:

> To my lovely and understanding
> aunt, Beatrice Wilkin.
>
> Cyclops

CHAPTER XVII

Paralyzing Light

BEATRICE WILKIN the aunt of Cyclops!

Everyone crowded around the small desk where Bess was seated and stared at the book she had found in the drawer.

"I can't believe it!" George burst out. "That prim little woman the aunt of a criminal!"

Nancy suggested that they look inside the book for further information. Everyone was astounded at the contents and puzzled as to why Miss Wilkin had left the book there.

"You would think," Professor Titus spoke up, "that she would want to conceal such information."

Bess sighed. "She probably forgot to take it with her because she was in such a hurry to get away."

As the group read on, there was only praise

for the elderly custodian who had permitted
Cyclops to sleep on the second floor of the museum and to carry on certain experiments in the
building.

"This means Cyclops is one person," Nancy
deduced, "not a gang."

"But what about his pals?" George spoke up.
"How much did they know?"

"Read this!" Nancy said presently. "Cyclops
actually experimented on the glowing eye project
right here, and Miss Wilkin knew all about it!"

George asked, "Do you suppose she could have
worked hand in hand with her nephew?"

"That seems incredible," Professor Titus replied. "I'm more inclined to think that Miss Wilkin did not understand the invention. When
several people inquired about it, she became suspicious herself. Then, after what happened to
Nancy yesterday, the woman panicked and left
suddenly."

Nancy was not completely satisfied with this
explanation. Did Miss Wilkin believe that Cyclops' pals were Emerson College students? Or
had she lied to Nancy and her friends when asked
about them?

The discussion was interrupted by a knock on
the front door. The professor opened it and admitted a man who said he was Ben Farley from
the telephone company.

"We've received complaints from people who

have tried to call here. Apparently your line's out of order."

Nancy pulled out the map of the museum's first floor and looked carefully for the main telephone-box location. She found it and the repairman suggested that the incoming line was probably underground in a basement not shown on the directions. Professor Titus and the girls went with him. They found the box.

"Uh-uh," the repairman said, "someone cut the line!"

After examining the break carefully, Farley asked, "Did you have a burglary?"

Professor Titus said he did not think so, but they had just discovered that an intruder had slept on the second floor.

The telephone man went out to his truck to get special wire and tools. The others returned to the lobby and continued to read the book of poems by Cyclops. There were many items which seemed to identify Cyclops as Zapp Crosson. One was a poem in which the words "cross" and "on" were used to describe an ill-tempered little boy with fiery red hair.

"He must have been describing himself as a child," George declared.

Nancy said she was sure Crosson would return to the museum and perhaps bring his pals with him. "I feel this place should be guarded," she said.

At once Professor Titus offered to stay.

"But not alone!" Nancy said. "I certainly think Bess and George and I should remain with you."

Just then the telephone repairman came back to the lobby and reported that service on the line had been restored.

"That's good," said Bess. "It's kind of eerie being in a place like this without a telephone."

Ben Farley smiled and said if there was any further trouble to contact the company. He drove off.

"The first person I should call," said Nancy, "is my dad."

Professor Titus said he would like to let his wife know the change of plan and why he would not be home.

Bess spoke up. "I think Burt and Dave should be told, too."

"Yes," George agreed, "and besides, we should find out if they have had any news of Ned either from him or from the authorities."

The calls were made. Burt and Dave were surprised and concerned for their friends' safety but thought the girls' plan to keep an overnight watch was a good one.

"We haven't heard anything from or about Ned," Burt added.

When all the phoning was finished, Bess glanced at her watch. "Do you know it's dinnertime?" she asked. "Suppose I phone a restaurant in town and see if they'll deliver some food to us?"

Hopefully she tried one place after another and was beginning to think the group would have to go all night without eating, when she found a roadside restaurant that did deliver meals. The food arrived within an hour. They sat on chairs in the main lobby to eat. After they finished, each one began to nod and close his eyes.

They took turns walking around, trying to stay awake. But by ten o'clock everyone was back in his chair and getting into a comfortable position for a nap.

All the lights had been turned out and the watchers remained silent until sleep overcame them.

No one knew how long they had dozed when suddenly the group was awakened by a strong, penetrating searchlight flashed in their faces. As the startled group concentrated on it, everyone realized that the light seemed to be emitted from a huge glowing eye.

Nancy's first thought was to make a dash for the person holding the searchlight. To her amazement she found herself unable to get up. She stared stupefied at the others. Each one sat paralyzed!

Suddenly a voice that seemed to come from far away said, "Don't try to follow me even after you can move again!"

"Don't follow me after you can move!"
the stranger ordered.

At once the huge light went out and the immobile group could vaguely hear the front door open and close. The person with the glowing eye searchlight had left!

It was fully five minutes before anyone could move or speak. Slowly Nancy arose and made her way to the telephone on the desk. As she lifted the phone, a light went on showing up the numbers. She dialed the police emergency number and got headquarters. A sergeant on duty promised to send men out right away.

Nancy turned on the lights in the lobby and asked the others how they were feeling. Fortunately no one had suffered any bad effects.

"That was a strange experience," Professor Titus remarked.

"Have you any explanation for it?" Nancy asked him.

"Not exactly," he replied, "but it reminds me of something I read about medical students studying the brain waves of a person who had been put to sleep under hypnosis. It was discovered that his wave pattern could be imprinted upon another brain by using a laser beam of a certain wavelength. Of course the original brain waves had to be programmed in order to be modulated. This in turn produced a 'paralyzing' sleep."

Nancy was thoughtful. "What happened to us must have been done some other way because nobody hypnotized us and the programming would have had to be different for each individual in the group."

"That's right," Professor Titus agreed. "The phenomenon we experienced will take a good deal of study."

Bess's eyes were wide open. "Who would ever think of such a horrible invention?"

Professor Titus smiled. "Criminals conjure up many things that ordinarily seem beyond their capabilities. I think I've made a discovery. The person who gave us the warning a few minutes ago sounded exactly like Zapp Crosson."

"Maybe he has been on the third floor all this time," George suggested. "I'll run up and see if that door leading to it is unlocked." In a couple of minutes she reported that the door was still tightly locked.

Bess looked frightened. "Are you saying that Zapp Crosson is up there with his paralyzing searchlight and may come back any time to use it on us again?"

Nancy said she doubted this because they had heard the front door close. "I don't think he'll return here for a while."

She picked up the phone once more and contacted police headquarters. This time she asked them to send out a detective, who was also a locksmith.

Ten minutes later a car with several officers reached the museum. One of them was Dr. Marcus, the police surgeon. He insisted upon examining each victim of the paralyzing searchlight.

He tested their responses and announced that the whole group was in good health. He asked them how they had felt during the immobile period. Professor Titus and the girls said they had had no unusual sensations except being unable to move.

"May we please go upstairs and watch you open the door?" Nancy asked the locksmith detective.

"Certainly," he answered. "My name is Tim Rooney."

The whole group trooped up the stairway and watched as the detective tried one key after another. Finally he was able to unlock the door.

The girls wanted to rush up to the top floor but Dr. Marcus said, "No, not until we find it's safe."

A few minutes later he came down. "It's okay. You're in for a surprise," he remarked. "There's a fully equipped electrical and electronic lab up there."

"How amazing!" said Professor Titus.

By this time Nancy had surmised as much. She led the way up the steps. What particularly drew her attention in the spacious attic room were a series of pictures on the walls. They depicted gruesome scenes of battles, both between individuals and groups, and the slaughter of animals.

"How ghastly!" Bess exclaimed.

By now everyone was staring at the pictures of persons and animals about to have one eye gouged out with various kinds of hand weapons.

Bess covered her eyes with her hands just as Dr. Marcus said, "The man who owns these pictures is an unusual and dangerous killer type."

Nancy's heart jumped. "And he is holding Ned—" She could not finish the sentence.

CHAPTER XVIII

Weird Heel Mark

"WHY, Nancy, you're white as a sheet!" Bess exclaimed. "What's the matter?"

"I was just thinking about what Crosson could do to Ned!"

George put an arm around her friend. "Please don't think the worst. I'm sure we'll capture that villain before he has a chance to do anything drastic." She went on to say that if Crosson were trying to get information out of Ned, he was not likely to kill him.

"But he might maim him," Nancy said with tears in her eyes. She buried her face in her hands and took a long, deep breath.

A few seconds later she raised her head and said, "You're absolutely right, George. I mustn't let my feelings overshadow my good sense."

She changed the subject by turning to Tim Rooney and asking if he would supply her with a key to the door leading to the attic.

He smiled and said, "You hope to trap the kidnapper right here in his own laboratory?"

Nancy nodded and Detective Rooney told her he would have a duplicate key made at once and bring it to her.

One of the other officers now asked Professor Titus and the girls to leave the attic. "We want to search this place thoroughly for the glowing eye searchlight," he said. "Also, there may be other dangerous gadgets here which we should remove."

Nancy and the others went to the main lobby. George asked Nancy, "What's our next assignment?"

The young detective replied, "I'd like to do some old-fashioned sleuthing. While Professor Titus guards the museum, how about the rest of us taking flashlights and magnifying glasses outdoors to search? We're pretty sure that Crosson was here tonight. Perhaps he left footprints."

The professor agreed. The girls took sleuthing equipment from pockets and handbags, then went outside to examine the grounds.

A few minutes later Nancy's eyes were fastened on a trail of footprints which her flashlight and magnifying glass had revealed.

"Look!" she cried out.

The cousins came to her side. They saw the prints and presently found an identical one deep in a soft spot.

"The heel mark is a copy of Cyclops' glowing eye!" Nancy exclaimed as she pointed to it.

Clearly pictured was the ugly face of a Cyclops, with an eye in the center of his forehead.

George asked, "Do you think this is a mark Crosson uses just for himself or is it the insignia for his pals, too?"

Nancy admitted she did not know. "But I'm going to tell the police about this mark."

The girls went back into the museum. They were just in time to meet the police officers coming from the attic.

"We found nothing dangerous," Tim Rooney reported, "so it will be all right for you to go up there, Miss Drew. But be very careful just the same."

"I have something to show you," Nancy spoke up. "It's outdoors. Please follow me to the side of the house."

She led the policemen to the spot where she had discovered the heel print. The men stared at it, perplexed.

One said, "This is very strange. I'll call headquarters and see if they have any data on a similar mark."

They all returned to the museum lobby and he made the call. After listening for over five minutes, the officer said, "I'll pass along the information. This is most interesting."

He put down the phone and explained that a long time ago a band of wizards was reported to have lived in Europe.

"These men pretended to be magicians. Actually they were a gang of thieves. They mesmerized anyone who got in the way of their activities."

"Perhaps," Nancy commented, "the wizards were able to cause a temporary paralysis in people, and that's where Crosson got his idea for the paralyzing eye."

The officer looked directly at Nancy. "Do you think your friend Ned Nickerson had anything to do with inventing the glowing eye?"

"No," she answered quickly. "I suspect that Ned was working on something else which he was keeping a secret, but Crosson found out what it was and tried to steal the invention. But so far Ned has refused to give it to Crosson."

Before anyone could comment, they heard a loud knock on the front door. One of the officers went to answer it. The caller proved to be Tim Rooney. He laughed and said, "You all look as if you expected a monster. I'm just plain old Tim Rooney."

George spoke up. "It wouldn't have surprised us if a monster had arrived. Actually we thought the caller might be a wizard."

"Where did you get that idea?" Mr. Rooney laughed.

Nancy told him what had been discovered during his absence. He was intrigued by the story of the ancient gang of wizards.

"I'm not one of them," he said, smiling, "although I have a reputation for being able to open any locked door with my special keys. Miss Drew, here's the key to the museum attic. Hope you catch your man real soon!"

The officers made a moulage of the strange heel print, and left after they had warned the group not to take any chances. The girls talked with Professor Titus for several minutes, then he walked into the room where the glowing eye had shone on the wall.

"Listen!" Bess said suddenly. "I hear a car coming!"

The girls wondered who was arriving. They felt sure it was not Crosson nor one of Cyclops' pals. A few seconds later there was a loud knock on the door. Nancy asked who was there.

Two male voices said, "Your guards for the night."

The girls burst out laughing. Burt and Dave!

Bess quickly pulled open the front door and the boys walked in.

Burt was grinning. "We thought you girls needed more protection."

Just then Professor Titus returned to the group. "So you boys didn't trust me to take care of them alone?" he asked, his eyes twinkling.

Burt and Dave knew he was teasing them, but they were a little embarrassed.

Dave said, "Sorry, Professor. Of course you could have done the job, but we'd kind of like to hang around."

"That's a lame explanation," the man replied, pretending to be as critical as he was sometimes known to be in his classroom.

Nancy spoke up. "Now that you boys are here, we'll put you to work. First, we'll tell you all about this evening's events, then give you jobs."

The two boys were astounded at the latest developments and Dave said, "As usual more things can happen to Nancy Drew and her friends in two hours than might happen in two years to somebody else."

The young detective smiled, then said, "Let's watch this museum closely. I suggest we divide forces and spread out."

"Good idea," Burt said. "Where do you want to station me?"

"Suppose you and I go to the attic," Nancy answered. "Wait until you see that fabulous laboratory!"

She went on to assign jobs to the others. Professor Titus and George were to station themselves near the panel where the glowing eye had been seen. "Bess and Dave, how about guarding the front door?"

The group quickly dispersed and went to their

individual posts. Nancy and Burt hurried upstairs to the second floor, then Nancy opened the attic door with the key she had just received. She flicked on the light switch and closed the door. Burt followed her up the steps and in a moment he was gazing in awe at the equipment.

Nancy, in the meantime, heard what sounded like a helicopter. Was it Crosson? She quickly turned off the light and told Burt to look out the window with her.

They could see a helicopter descending in the field behind the museum!

"Burt, I'll bet it's Crosson!" Nancy exclaimed.

Together they watched the whirlybird. Both had the same thought: Was it the robot craft which had landed on Nancy's front lawn in River Heights?

"Maybe Crosson and Ned are in it!" Burt suggested.

The helicopter settled to the ground but instantly went up again. It circled for a few minutes, then took off.

"Maybe someone dropped out," Nancy remarked.

"And he may come into the museum!" Burt added.

Just then they heard a scream from the first floor!

CHAPTER XIX

The Captive

Who had screamed? Someone in their group or an intruder?

Nancy was torn between two theories: the cry might have come from Bess who had been frightened, but on the other hand an intruder might have screamed purposely to lure Burt and herself from the attic. Regardless, she felt that they should investigate.

"Suppose I go," Nancy suggested. "You wait here in case Crosson or one of his pals climbs in a window or comes out of a secret hiding place."

Nancy tiptoed down the attic steps. She opened the door warily and gazed into the dark hall. There was not a sound and to her this seemed ominous.

As she stood debating whether or not to descend to the first floor, she noticed a small flicker of light. In a moment she realized that someone was coming up the steps. She could not see the person's face, but she could distinguish the outline of a man. In one hand he held the paralyzing glowing eye searchlight. Its beams had been turned low.

"I'd better make up my mind what I'm going to do," Nancy thought.

A moment later a distressing thought came to her. Maybe her friends on the first floor had been paralyzed again by the glowing eye searchlight!

"The same thing will happen to me if I go near it!"

Quickly she stepped back onto the attic stairway and closed the door. Ascending on tiptoe as rapidly as possible, she went at once to Burt's side and whispered:

"Cyclops may be on his way up here with his paralyzing light. We'd better hide."

"And also try to figure out how we're going to capture him," Burt said, "without being paralyzed ourselves."

Their flashlights turned on, the two moved quietly around the lab looking for something they could use to capture the man. Nancy noticed a long black cloth in one corner of the lab and picked it up. It proved to be a perforated sack.

"That is just the thing to pull over that villain's head!" Burt remarked. "It'll stop him but it won't smother him."

Nancy agreed and said she thought their best

hiding place would be somewhere behind the door of the closet where bottles of chemicals were kept. By leaving the door ajar, they could watch the person's actions. By now someone was climbing the steps to the attic. Nancy and Burt waited breathlessly.

When he reached the lab he at once turned up the beam of his searchlight and cast it over the room. Nancy and Burt could not be seen and were safe from its harmful rays. Burt clutched the sack and watched the intruder dim his searchlight.

In the crack of light shining into the closet, Burt held up a finger and crooked it to form the letter C. He followed with an R. Nancy realized that he was spelling Crosson!

She and Burt waited for their chance. Crosson walked closer and closer to the closet. Just before reaching it, he turned his back on the door. This was Burt and Nancy's opportunity to capture him!

Like lightning they sprang from the closet. Burt pulled the sack over the man's head, while Nancy held his arms tightly to his sides. The movement startled Crosson so much that he fell and dropped the searchlight. Fortunately its beams had been diverted from Burt and Nancy. Nancy reached out and with one foot shut off the power.

By now Burt had managed to tie the lower part

of the sack around the man's waist. The prisoner struggled to get away. His muscles were strong. Nancy realized that he must be bound more securely. She snapped on the ceiling light and looked for something with which to bind their prisoner. She found a coil of electric wire and tied the man's ankles tightly, while Burt tried hard to keep the sack over his head and his arms pinned down. Next, Nancy wound the rest of the wire about his body so he could not free himself.

"Let me out of here!" the prisoner screamed.

Burt looked at Nancy who nodded, and the sack was taken from Crosson's head. Nancy thought she had never seen an angrier, more calculating smirk on anyone's face. The man's fiery red hair was sticking out in all directions. His eyes were like two gleaming coals, as hatred shone in them.

"Let me go!" he shouted.

Nancy looked at him and asked, "Where's Ned Nickerson?"

Instead of answering, Crosson cried out, "You'd better release me or you'll all die!"

Since the man was unable to use either his arms or legs, Nancy and Burt were sure that the threat was only an idle one. Nancy said she would go to the first floor and get Professor Titus to identify Crosson. Upon hearing this, Crosson's eyes closed to a mere slit. Nancy thought he looked like a tiger about to spring upon its prey.

She hurried from the room and ran to the lobby. The scene before her startled the young detective. It was evident that Bess, George, Dave, and Professor Titus had received a dose from the paralyzing searchlight. Fortunately they were all regaining their ability to move.

"Zapp Crosson is our prisoner in the attic!" Nancy exclaimed. "Professor Titus, will you go up there with me to identify him?"

"Yea!" shouted Dave.

"Hypers!" George said. "You've done it again, Nancy Drew!"

The young detective still looked sober. "He won't answer my question about where Ned is, but I'm going back to see if I can find out anything." Then she asked, "Tell me exactly what happened down here."

Bess explained that she had seen the front door open silently and the red-haired Cyclops had come in with his paralyzing searchlight and immediately beamed it on Dave and her, but she had managed to scream. George and Professor Titus had come running, and in turn had received an electrical shock.

Not only Professor Titus, but Bess, George, and Dave accompanied Nancy to the attic. The professor took one look at the prisoner and said, "It's Zapp Crosson all right."

Then he glanced at the turned-off searchlight which was still lying on the floor. He picked it up and examined the strange gadget. It would no longer switch on and he declared that the mechanism had worn out.

Nancy went to stand in front of the prisoner. Again she asked, "Where's Ned Nickerson?"

Crosson eyed her skeptically. "Let me loose and I'll tell you a lot," he replied.

The others waited for him to give an explanation about the kidnapping. Instead he suddenly began to laugh.

"I know you're going to have me arrested but the authorities have no charge on which to hold me. You have no proof of anything. I had permission to stay in this museum and to work in this laboratory. That's not against the law. I'll deny everything else I'm accused of. That goes for your boy friend, Nancy Drew. I happen to know he's safe, but he'll never be able to leave the place where he's being held unless I give the word."

The red-haired man stopped speaking and refused to answer any further questions. When Nancy realized that for her to continue was hopeless, she decided to call the police and turn the whole matter over to them.

She hurried to the first floor and dialed the number. Tim Rooney answered.

"Don't tell me you've caught the intruder!" he said.

"Yes, I'm reporting just that," Nancy replied. "But he won't tell where Ned Nickerson is. Can some of your men come to the museum at once and take charge?"

"They'll be there shortly," Tim Rooney told her, then said how astounded he was that Nancy Drew had caught the kidnapper.

When two other officers arrived, they were equally amazed. Nancy led them at once to the third-floor laboratory. Crosson glared at the officers and instantly told the men that they had no case against him.

"I demand that you release me!" he said.

"There's already a warrant out for your arrest," one of the officers told him. "And if we need any proof, I think there are several witnesses right here in this room who will testify against you in court."

The men searched the prisoner's pockets. When they found nothing, they untied the electric cord which had bound him, slipped on handcuffs, and let Crosson stand.

"We'll lock him up," one officer said. Turning to Nancy, he asked, "Just how did you solve this case?"

"By two 1923 pennies," the young detective replied. Crosson gave a start and cast an ugly look in Nancy's direction.

The officer asked, "Where will I be able to find you people?"

Professor Titus said he thought the group should return to Emerson at once for a good night's sleep. Everyone agreed and the police were given the telephone number of the fraternity house.

By the time they reached Emerson it was daybreak. The whole group tumbled into bed, exhausted.

"What a day!" Bess said as she closed her eyes and trailed off to sleep.

George immediately followed her cousin, but after Nancy had relaxed for half an hour without dozing off, her mind began to race. She wished that Ned had been rescued instead of Crosson having been captured.

"We'll have to start another big search," she said to herself.

Presently the young detective became so restless she decided to get up, dress, and walk around the campus. Maybe a long stroll would help her figure out what her next move should be. She went outside and crossed the campus to a large playing field.

Hearing a noise above her, she looked up and saw a helicopter coming. As Nancy watched it, she was startled to see the craft pause directly overhead, then begin to descend.

Her heart pounding, she asked herself, "Is this the robot copter? And if so, why is it coming here?"

Suddenly it occurred to Nancy that one or more of Crosson's pals might be aboard! Should she run and avoid being captured?

The young detective was too intrigued to leave. The helicopter might contain another message from Ned!

CHAPTER XX

Surprising Story

As the helicopter descended closer to Nancy, she became more and more tense. The craft settled to the ground.

The rotors slowed down and finally stopped. As Nancy stared, the door opened and the pilot jumped out. Suddenly Nancy caught her breath, then she started to run toward the young man as fast as she could.

"Ned! Ned! I can't believe it!" she cried out.

Realizing who she was, Ned too began to run. A few moments later they were in each other's arms.

"Oh, Nancy, I'm so glad you were the first one to greet me on my homecoming!"

"Ned, you're safe!" she exclaimed. This brought a twinkle to the good-looking young man's brown eyes. "There's so much to find out

about where you've been," Nancy continued.
"And how did you ever get away from where
Crosson had hidden you?"

Ned looked at Nancy unbelievingly. "You
found out who my abductor was?"

By this time Nancy and Ned were walking arm
in arm toward the fraternity house.

"I've been working on the case. Last night we
captured Zapp Crosson and he's in jail now."

"Thank goodness for that," Ned replied. "I
don't think I could have taken much more.
Crosson grew nuttier all the time and I was afraid
he would kill me. Oh, you wanted to know where
he has kept me hidden lately and how I got
away."

"I know it wasn't the farmhouse nor the cabin
in the swampy wilderness because the police are
watching both places," Nancy said.

"You arranged that?" he asked.

Nancy told him that she had been working
with Bess, George, Burt, and Dave. "And Professor Titus was very helpful, too."

Ned revealed that Crosson had a third hideout.
It was on an abandoned army post with a level
but rather overgrown flying field.

"Whenever Crosson took me any place, I paid
strict attention to how and where he piloted the
copter. A couple of times he let me fly it.

"Last evening a friend of his came and took

Crosson away in the copter—I think to the Anderson Museum—but only the friend returned with the craft."

"Where is he now?" Nancy asked.

Ned said that the man had gone off in his car after giving him some supper.

"I asked him how long Crosson would be away, and he said at least a couple of days. That gave me an idea. Crosson had not chained me as tightly as he had at the other two places and after a while I was able to get loose. I determined to try flying the copter, but I didn't dare set it down in any airport. I know I was breaking aviation rules. However, due to the circumstances I'm sure I won't have any trouble with the authorities."

"Was the glowing eye his own invention?"

"Yes, and he experimented with it in several ways—making it turn red, using a paralyzing type in a searchlight, and trying out a miniature, indestructible one. But he put a speaking tape in it, so if anyone should pick up the eye and open the lid, it would sound a warning. Crosson didn't want anyone to discover his secret. He also magnetized the inner wall below where the big eye appeared in the museum. It was put there to trap anyone investigating the spot."

"I know," said Nancy. "It happened to me."

"What!" Ned exclaimed. "That scoundrel!

Well, I'm glad he couldn't finish his invention. He needed mine to perfect his own for commercial uses."

"Oh, I'm so glad he never got it," Nancy said. "Ned, what about the eye that glowed on one of your notes? Who put it there?"

"The paper was from a pad of Crosson's."

"And the drawing on the paper at your home that was eye-shaped and had numbers on it?" Nancy said.

Ned grinned. "That was my secret. Sometime I'll explain it to you."

"Tell me, how did Crosson happen to adopt the name Cyclops?" Nancy asked.

"He became interested in the origin of the word and made his invention in the shape of a huge eye. Then he decided to call himself Cyclops. When I sent the note to you, I didn't dare use his real name in case he found it. I also thought Cyclops might be a good clue for you."

By this time the couple had reached the fraternity house. Though it was early, several students were up. When Ned walked in the door, they stared at him as if he were a creature from another planet. Then a great cheer went up.

The noise awakened everyone else in the house and within minutes Bess, George, Burt, and Dave were surrounding Ned, shaking hands or kissing him and asking a hundred questions.

"Tell you what, fellows—and girls," Ned said, winking at Nancy, George, and Bess, "suppose we have breakfast, and while we're eating, I'll tell you everything that happened to me. Now I want to call my parents. Nancy, will you call the police?"

"Yes, and tell them you're safe."

After assuring Mr. and Mrs. Nickerson he was all right, and promising to see them that evening, Ned went to his room and had the first really good shower he had taken since leaving Emerson. Refreshed, he came downstairs and all the students and visitors and Professor Titus, whom Burt had invited, assembled in the dining room. Ned ate some fruit and cereal, then got up and began his story.

"As you know, I worked next to Zapp Crosson in the lab. He proved to be a very inquisitive person and was always looking at my notes and watching my experiments. Quite accidentally I hit upon something which I think will be a worthwhile invention.

"Crosson thought so too and secretly determined to steal it from me. At one point I became a little suspicious, so I gathered up all my formulas and notes relating to my project and mailed them to my home."

"But what about the helicopter sketches that were in the same package?" Nancy interrupted.

"Crosson used to draw copters all the time. He

left a sheet of them on my worktable one day. It must have become mixed in with my own papers."

Ned paused a moment before continuing his story. "He fooled me part of the time. Though I was suspicious of his intentions regarding my invention, I did not suspect he planned to kidnap me and keep me a prisoner until he could get my invention and market it.

"A week ago yesterday Crosson came to my room and told me he had a copter which he kept, with special permission, on a farm outside of town. He asked me if I would like to take a ride in it. He seemed so friendly that I was taken off guard and accepted. I had no time to write a note to Burt and Dave, because he insisted we leave at once.

"We drove out to the farm and I left the car parked at the side of the road. Everything went well until we got into the copter. Then Crosson suddenly pulled a gun and said I was his prisoner and he would not release me until I had given him a complete set of drawings and formulas for my invention. Of course I refused and he took me to that wilderness hideout."

"How wicked!" Bess Marvin burst out. Other students agreed and there was a few minutes of bitter talk about the graduate student. Finally Ned went on to relate what else had happened to him.

"Every time Crosson got word from his pals that the police were on his trail, he moved me. I had an idea it was Nancy who was keeping the police informed. We went from place to place but they were always in secluded areas.

"In the beginning Crosson wanted to scare Nancy off the case so she wouldn't try to solve it. Apparently he knew of your reputation, Nancy, and also where you lived. He said he could make his copter into a robot and that he intended to program it to go directly to your house. He was planting a bomb inside it, which was to roll out when the door opened automatically and blow up part of your home, and he even hoped to injure you and your father so you'd be too scared to try finding me."

"A bomb!" George exclaimed. "Nothing went off and the police didn't see it in the copter. What happened to it?"

Ned smiled and said that he had talked Crosson into letting him walk outside to see the helicopter when it was ready.

"I had decided to send Nancy a warning note so I wrote it and put the note into my pocket. When Crosson had everything set to go, I told him I'd heard something in the sky. Maybe somebody was coming after us. Of course he looked up and this gave me a chance to remove the bomb and put the note into the copter."

"What did you do with the bomb?" Burt spoke up.

Ned said he had taken a chance and hidden it under his coat. The robot copter was taking off from the hiding place in the wilderness.

"After it had gone, I told Crosson I wanted to get a certain plant out of the swamp and he assumed it had something to do with my invention, because he felt sure I was going to give in to his demands. He didn't want to walk into the mucky area himself, so he told me to go ahead but warned me not to try to escape. I assured him I wouldn't, but went far enough away so that he couldn't see what I was doing. I bent down to pull up a plant, but at the same time I gently placed the bomb underwater." Ned laughed. "I suppose it's still there. We must tell the police about it."

As Ned paused, Dave asked, "When Crosson found out the bomb didn't arrive at the Drew home, what did he think?"

"That during the flight the bomb must have rolled out and dropped off some place. Crosson watched the newspapers to see if there was a report of any accident but he never saw one."

Ned told his listeners that when the robot copter did not return to the wilderness hideout, Crosson decided to go see what had happened. "It was he who knocked out the police guard at the Drew house, cut the rope which had been used to tie the helicopter down, and flew the craft back where we were staying."

After glancing at his wristwatch, Ned announced, "Fellows, it's time for those of you who have classes to leave. Later I'll tell you more about my abduction."

Nancy and her special friends went to the guest room and sat down. Fortunately Burt and Dave had no classes so they could stay to hear the rest of Ned's story. They learned that Crosson had robbed the Emerson lab to equip his own in the wilderness. Also that he had set the bomb in the file drawer of duplicate papers relating to the glowing eye. He didn't want anyone to see them.

Nancy asked, "Ned, is your invention still a secret, or could you tell us about it now?"

"I sure can, especially after all the great things you have done for me and captured Cyclops. My invention is a new way for a scientist to produce laser light so that even a small source of energy will do great feats. It's done by converting all of the energy into light."

"How wonderful!" Nancy exclaimed, feeling particularly proud of her friend.

George agreed, also Burt and Dave.

Bess made no comment for several seconds, then she said, "Ned, your invention sounds marvelous but it's about as clear as mud to me!"

The others laughed and it was agreed that Ned

would have to go into a far deeper explanation in order to make them fully understand his invention.

Before the group broke up, they learned from Ned that Crosson controlled the glowing eye in the museum from his lab there. "His pals, who pretended to be Emerson students, had helped him take it down but left all the active wires," Ned explained. "By the way, I have the names of all Crosson's pals. I'll turn them over to the police. Crosson himself by accident left a paper with the word Cyclops written in Greek among my drawings. He told me this a few days ago, thinking it was a good joke, but he never had a chance to steal the material because I came into the lab just then and he had to put everything back in my file in a hurry. That very day I mailed all my work home, also the papers I kept in my room here."

As Nancy walked to her room, she felt a combination of happiness at Ned's return and a kind of sinking feeling which always came over her when a mystery was solved.

But she did not have long to wait for *The Secret of the Forgotten City* to come along and involve her in another exciting adventure.

Now, with Crosson in jail and Ned back, Nancy decided to call her father and tell him the good news. She went at once to the phone and called his office.

When the lawyer heard the astonishing report, he said, "Congratulations, Nancy! I had a feeling all along you could solve the mystery of the Anderson Museum, which, of course, turned out to be much more than that. By the way, I never did tell you how the case came to me. A large donor to the museum saw the glowing eye and wondered if his money was being spent unwisely. He asked me to find out. I'll phone him that Nancy Drew found the answer!"

After a little more conversation with her father, Nancy felt she should tell Marty King that Crosson was in jail and Ned was home. She said to her father, "I'd like to speak to Marty."

There was a pause, then Mr. Drew said, "She's no longer working here."

"Oh!" Nancy exclaimed. "She left?"

"Well, yes, but to be truthful, Nancy, I asked her to resign. Her legal work was excellent, but I began to realize that she was always arranging my business affairs so that she and I would have to eat luncheon or dinner together. Then I learned how jealous she was of you and your accomplishments."

Nancy was smiling to herself and delighted that Marty King had left her father's employ.

"Nancy dear, I may as well tell you the whole story," her father went on. "I'm embarrassed about it, but what brought on my asking Marty to leave was"—there was a long pause—"when Marty asked me to marry her!"

Nancy took a deep breath. For a couple of seconds she was not sure what to say to her father. This was a situation which she had never encountered before. Finally she decided to make light of the whole matter.

"Dad," she said, "if you ever want to find me a new mother, please promise me she won't be someone who tries to solve my mysteries!"

Her father laughed heartily. "I promise," he said.

Own the original 58 action-packed
HARDY BOYS MYSTERY STORIES®
In *hardcover* at your local bookseller OR
Call 1-800-788-6262, and start your collection today!

All books priced @ $5.99

Own the original 56 thrilling

NANCY DREW MYSTERY STORIES®

In *hardcover* at your local bookseller OR
Call 1-800-788-6262, and start your collection today!

All books priced @ $5.99